THROUGH JADED EYES
RYAN W. McCLELLAN

Circle 5 Publishing Group
9835 SW 84th Street, Miami FL 33173

ISBN: 978-1-727017-052

Dedicated to my grandfather, Samuel Zolotin...

*Your wisdom will never be forgotten, and
without you I would have never known my
talent as a writer. I will never forget your love
and the lessons you taught me...*

"How many of you know the sixteen words in President Bush's State of the Union address that led us to war? How many know my wife's name? Now how can you know one and not the other? When did the question move from 'why are we going to war' to 'who is this man's wife?' I asked the first question, but somebody else asked the second, and it worked, because none of us know the truth. The offense that was committed was not committed against me; it was not committed against my wife. It was committed against you — all of you. And if that makes you angry, or feel misrepresented, do something about it.

When Benjamin Franklin left Independence Hall just after the second drafting, he was approached by a woman on the street. The woman said, "Mr. Franklin, what manner of government have you bequeathed us?" Franklin said: "A Republic, madam, if you can keep it." The responsibility of a country is not in the hands of a privileged few. We are strong, and we are free from tyranny as long as each one of us remembers his or her duty as a citizen. Whether it's to report a pothole at the top of your street, or lies in the State of the Union address, speak out! Ask those questions; demand that truth! Democracy is not a free ride, man, I'm here to tell ya. But this is where we live, and if we do our job, this is where our children will live. God bless ya."bb- "The Zurchin"

PREFACE

This book started off as twelve short stories, most of which were written when I was sixteen years of age. I have been writing my entire life, but this story is by far the most important among thousands of others. That is because this book quite literally predicted the future. Bear in mind that most of the concept was established prior to the recession of 2008, and lightyears before ISIS, terrorist attacks on nations abroad, and America's fading epidemic of school shootings. In this sense, you will notice a number of these facets are broad and symbolic in nature, found within the pages you are about to read.

Remember that we all have a duty to do what is best for not only ourselves, but those who walk among us. When you read this book, remember that the paradigm shift brought forth by the main character was never meant to denote what is actually going on around us today. This is the updated version of the original book, of which was officially completed in 2011, prior to Sandy Hook and many of today's most frightening issues. I hope you find a calm yet lucid sense of discomfort when you read this. Why would I want my readers to be uncomfortable? It is because that is where we are most likely to find solutions, of which was the point of this in the first place. Benjamin Franklin once said: "Progress is born from agitation. It is agitation or stagnation."

By that he meant: no great prospect is bound through being content; in order to facilitate a change – whether good or bad – we must find out what is wrong before we propose a reasonable solution. And in this case, that feeling of disgust in your stomach as you read the words that proceed this introduction should serve as a reminder that the world is not safe, and that our future as a country (and a world in generality) is doomed to walk a thousand years of darkness if we do not find a way to rectify our wrongdoings. We cannot prevent school shootings; we cannot prevent fanaticism and terrorist attacks. But we can look for solutions; we can try and find a guiding light in the darkest of places, and I hope this serves as a reminder that we are not safe; we never have been.

And that is why this book calls upon so many facets of daily life: fear of fear itself, and the oncoming storm of political backlash that will begin a paradigm shift toward either a better world, or one worth nothing but a burning Cross and a prayer for those who have died protecting us from harm (only to find that said harm is unstoppable). Thank you for getting this far into the book, and please make sure you read the entire epitaph.

Admittedly, the first several pages may be confusing; you may not fully understand what I am getting at until halfway through. So, give it a chance. Do not let confusion drive you away from continuing through the entire story, as you will not be let down. Again, this was originally a culmination of several short stories that were syndicated into a single novel. You have no idea how hard it is to form a solid plot based on conjecture. As of the republishing of this novel, I had to copy and paste the original Word document because I lost the original copy.

So, I hope you find this welcoming, and something worth reading over and over again. And remember, judge a book by its cover as often as you must, for the cover is merely a symbol for what lies within.

Thank you for your time.

CHAPTER ONE

Some people (the lucky ones, anyway) will carry on through their entire existence without ever encountering a war, and I can count on knowing that there will always be people who feel that simply because an individual has not crossed paths with conflict, automatically suggests that their world is one of peace. I've lived my entire life seeing many wars, either in present tense or past, in Junior High textbooks where we idolize false deities for crimes against man. Though I can guarantee to you one thing, and it is a promise I will make to you, the reader, as though we may not know each other, we carry the same weight; we hold the same breath, and it is not to be ignored. It is something much more unsettling than war, and it is simply: bad peace.

If you take the time to truly analyze the unpredictable nature of a war, you'll develop within yourself a thick-enough layer of callous across your ethical spectrum that will make it easier to clearly see the supplementary details of what a war does to the human race as a whole. You'll begin to see how little the views of an individual actually matter when it comes down to picking a side to fight for; you'll see how little it matters who was right or who was wrong, as long as your side is right, and their side is wrong; and you'll see how little actually changes when the war is over - both sides will remain unspoken enemies. The only difference is, now one nation feels its victory was one of omnipotence, while the other is afraid that their enemy may be right in their thinking.

War was back when the individual accepted fear as a tool for survival. It was an emotion; it was a feeling; it was intrinsic and instrumental at the same time – it had self-value. Naturally, the human race found ways to deal with it, and I guess during this time people were ultimately in touch with themselves on the inside. But you must understand that a lot changes about a species when it begins to question its instincts and emotions, as well as its infrastructure as a whole. With a question follows in its footsteps the tiresome pursuit for a logical, rational answer. And when no answer is found (regardless of how profanely stupid the question may be), the arteries of a worrisome nation begin to tighten around the neck, until the frustration bleeds through the flesh and our species resorts to doing what it does best.

To stumble upon the absence of logic and rationality, and only for a species as stubborn in its ways as ours, is to stumble upon a breeding ground for regrets and wrongdoings. So we began to manipulate, until we found a solution, regardless of how fabricated it may have been, or how little sense it made when taken into context. Us humans, we are bred and raised on the systematic and the formulas, never the emotions or the feelings, and as time had progressed to a point in our poignant existence where feelings and emotions were invalidated by technology and innovation, there was no room for even an unsolved question.

It was then that fear no longer operated through two jaded eyes as an emotion and an instinct, but rather a disease, and to attempt to cure something so utilitarian as fear is absolutely absurd in nature and perhaps one of the only things the human scientific population has no ability to treat, only eliminate.

Unfortunately, this was the type of thinking that led to the eventual extermination of an entire generation, and a war that would scar the world for the remainder of its existence. It was the last war this world would ever see, and the turning point in human history that ultimately led to what the generations to come would call "The Great Degeneration": a period of time in which human civilization essentially found a way within its confounding infrastructure to successfully eradicate, singularly, its many technological advances, scientific merit and achievement.

To summarize: thousands of years of progress as a world became utterly obsolete and slowly but surely deteriorated. A world without fear is a world without control, and a world without control won't last for very long. It was a dream held accountable by many scientists of their time: to eliminate an emotion – an emotion accountable for death and destruction time and time again. But because medicine had detracted to a point where research was not within proper means, there was only one way to properly eliminate such a "disease".

In this world, there is only one accurate method our civilization can use to determine who is among the fearless, the cured, and who holds the very pulse of the Sickness, and thus must be eliminated (by its own blood-soaked hand). Though this time, it was not an ordinary citizen that was being "tested", and tension was, without a doubt, extremely high, even more so than usual. "You know the rules: you get one bullet each. Two will enter the arena. Only one will leave," barked the loud horn.

"Commence the Manhattan Square Vaccination..."

CHAPTER TWO

The colors bled together like wet paint on canvas and every movement fell into slow motion, as Robert Sathers raced through hallway after hallway, the predator and the prey. He was his last line of defense and his first line of fire, his bodyguard and his fatal enemy if his Sickness bled through. If he feared, if he let the adrenaline break free from his command, he would be the victim in an unforgiving game of foxhunt.

Suddenly, he felt the air around him break free from his control as his foot lodged its way into a stump of concrete and he flew forward, a second's airborne and a flying target if his enemy were near enough to see. Luckily this game had just begun, and hopefully his enemy was face down in a puddle on the other side, as well. No time to think or wonder.

"Get up."

He forced his way onto tired knees and next, his feet, stumbling amidst the sea of gravity around him and finally finding his balance.

"Now Run."

He flew forward, rising like a phoenix from the ashes,

as he raced through a former empire he had never known, surrounded by the flurry and the chaos of the ruins he was entombed between: former Manhattan, twenty years following The Great Degeneration.

It was nothing but a grayscale of its former self, a tomb of concrete and shards of metal, shattered bridges and blown-out concrete buildings, and the rubble-littered alleyway in which he now raced through, not with any destination but a simple mission: kill or be killed. He reached a dead-end as he turned a corner. "Fuck," he muttered.

He needed to keep moving, obstacles or not, or he was de-

Four things happened over the period of the next two seconds before he could even finish his thought. One, a single gunshot rang from behind him, cracking the silence in the air like a whip. Two, he ducked to his knees in a flurry of primal gut instinct - anything to make himself a smaller target for that one airborne bullet. Three, he pivoted on his heels and turned to face his opponent. With a single inhale, he aligned the gun to face its target, and he pulled the trigger. And four, the bullet left its chamber with a crack, and everything fell back to reality.

The man in the distance had the same reaction to the gunshot: he ducked, which was morbidly unfortunate, as the gun had been aligned toward its target's chest, and as he lowered his body to the ground in an effort to dodge the bullet, he placed his face within the line of fire, catching the bullet in his eye and blowing the temporal lobe clean out the back of its skull encasing. The lifeless body fell climactically to the ground in a heap of dead weight. The blood began to pour from the wide-open gash, and it encircled his corpse.

And that was it. "Two bullets, one man left standing." A smirk overtook the winner's face, and he began a slow pace towards the body of his victim, laughing silently under his breath and twirling his gun on the peak of his finger. He stopped inches from the shattered head, letting the blood encircle his shoes. Before he could release his breath, the floor was swiftly painted with his own blood as gunshots rang all around him, bullets ricocheting off of the concrete walls and ground as they penetrated his body. He fell to his knees and collapsed next to his adversary, and their blood ran together.

Suddenly there was no loser and there was no winner; just two dead bodies and one pool of spilt blood. The soldiers lowered their guns, and a man appeared from the side of the chaos, dressed neatly in a pressed black suit and a white tie, his hands in his pockets and disappointment clearly evident on his face. He stopped to face the two corpses and kicked the side of the one who would have walked away clean if he hadn't made one single mistake, in a world where fear meant death.

"The fucking coward...he shouldn't have ducked."

*   *   *

After the failure and resulting eradication of Admiral Sathers' son during the Manhattan Square Vaccination, it was made entirely certain that the night's events would be dragged silently above the reach of the public and sealed tightly between its coffin walls. The incident was to be kept only between the blind eyes and deaf ears of those trained to never speak and never think; those who had undergone the baptisms of gunpoint indoctrination. Claus Sathers (Admiral) was a highly-respected and an equally well-renowned member of the "TRITE" ("To Revolt Is To Evolve") Movement: the organization that stood at the head of the societal hierarchy, and the leading supporter of The Cure.

They were the first of the many factions that formed during the aftermath of The Great Degeneration, and the last to falter in the face of adversity. They were the bloodstained hands that danced the puppet strings; they were the conniving, controlling voices as to which a nation listened with open ears, repeating every syllable silently and devoutly, never questioning why or how; they were the Government, the Senate, the Congress, the Army, the Media, the President, the Design and the Control, and they were never wrong. But to maintain control, you must have the control to maintain. A society cleansed of fear is a society in which the hands of power cannot threaten by simply wielding a blade; they must use it. The psychology behind this can best be set into ink by the fore founding father of the TRITE revolution:

"Sheep will follow because it is in their nature to do so – They have no other way of thinking or acting – It is instinctive to them. In contrast, it is in the nature of the human to think for itself – It has the power to build its own path – It will only follow if it wants to. Tell the human he will be killed if he does not follow, and he will follow – Fear is control. Because fear is instinctive, it only depends on how deep the blade must push through the skin before nature takes over. It is then that you have the human stupefied to the level of the sheep, and all you have to do is lead the herd." And the theory was quite accurate.

When you remove fear from a creature as clever and capable of destruction as the human, you are tilling the grounds upon which chaos and upheaval are bred. But regardless of what you are raised to believe (i.e. that fear is a cancer and must be restrained), the being will ultimately regress to its primitive instincts if the blade is pushed deep enough. TRITE was the definitive hand that held the knife.

To sum it up: society was fearless, but they were not stupid. TRITE maintained their control by manipulating its peoples' beliefs, and their system for doing so was complex in nature yet simple in act: whenever someone got out of line, they made it in their best interest to dig as deep as needed in order to unleash the primitive fear within all of us that can never be washed away by what we believe - instinct rules over conviction. In essence, the rest of the world saw the torture as "infection" rather than what it truly was, and this kept them in line; no one wanted to step out of contour because they believed TRITE had the power to "infect" them, and who would ever dare wish to be infected?

They had found a paradox among the theories set

forth by their fore founding members: a way to maintain control even within the boundaries of a society that believed fear was a disease, and they were the only ones who knew that they were doing it.

It was the ultimate method of brainwashing; it was clean, efficient, and required very little effort. When you do things right, people will not be sure if you have done anything at all. All that was required was a constant state of fear among the city, while at the same time: providing a well-oriented reason to "fear" in the first place.

Power such as this is expected to maintain its authority, integrity, and above all: its fearlessness. A powerful figure revealed to have a son who failed the Manhattan Square Vaccination was a ticking time bomb, and it was made sure to remain distant from prying eyes. But another ticking time bomb was in the making, as the uncontrollable forces of nature steadied their pistols and found their triggers...

CHAPTER THREE

The tow truck was on its way down 87th, the defective Corolla strapped to its back like dead weight. Just five minutes prior, it was under the confiscation and careful watch of the New Manhattan Bomb Squad, but it was released when all traces of explosives were declared as faulty. They never bothered in removing the C4 cartridges; they were so vacantly defective to the naked eye that they were better off destroyed with the car than separately.

It seemed almost too coincidental, though no one ever successfully connected the two deadly events, when the tow truck made a left on 98th and for only a brief moment, it fell within mere feet of the esteemed Admiral Sathers of the TRITE Foundation, in his vehicle, on his way back from the Manhattan Square Vaccination of his own son, and on the car's built-in phone discussing the failed terrorist bomb scare.

"Sounds like someone's trying to shock us into chaos..."

And somewhere in a building above, a voice broke the silence: "Perfect," and in a sweat-soaked hand a red button was pressed.

The C4 explosives left inside the Corolla detonated, a plan so calculated and timed so precisely that the two vehicles were close enough to blow each other clear off of the street. Shrapnel rained down upon the asphalt and in an instant it was all over in a fiery blaze.

No one ever caught the man who pushed that button, and no one ever truly knew what happened in that instance, except a single man, who successfully placed a bomb within a foot of the President and set it off.

*   *   *

The people of a fearless nation never saw the backlash as the tide began to rise. It was an explosion in the heart of a busy city street that began what would be the eventual collapse of an entire empire. The cause was never found – terrorists, rebellion, an overheated car – it did not matter, because it was regardless of who began the fire. It was how they tried to put it out. In a fraction of a second – that which followed the explosion, the city - suddenly faced with a situation as alien to them as the thought of fear an emotion – felt their hearts jump into their throats.

"What was that?!" a voice broke the silence – a deafening sense of fractured time that seemed to spread with the smoke. "There's a fire!" another voice, female. It was in this chaotic instance - this concise interlude of disorder and disarray - that a sickness built from control would fail to be controlled, and a nerve was to be struck. The smoke began to clear, enough so for visibility's sake, revealing the damage done. It was not a pretty sight.

"He's hurt! Call an ambulance!" A crowd was slowly beginning to gather, onlookers gazing from afar, thrown from their daily tasks into what would become the final breath to break free of TRITE's control, and their eyes were the culprits. It was unfortunate that their destinies would lie at the end of three cocked-and-loaded rifles.

Among the crowd that had gathered laid an elderly man, his leg severed and his eyes slowly fading from consciousness, the only signs of life his slurred screams of pain. His body was charred beyond recognition. As a woman dialed for an ambulance on her cell phone, control broke the silence through the ashes.

"Freeze!" a commanding growl from afar. "You're under arrest in the sanctity of 'Plaguata Armada" (a fancy way of being taken into captivity for being "Sick"). The TRITE officers were quick to respond to situations such as this, though they were never quite prepared. It took less than a minute for the three gun-toting officers to appear from beyond the ashes, their polished M-16s raised and aimed square at the heads of the unlucky citizens of a sadist nation weaned on mistrust and violence. Those with the decency to help an injured civilian were now staring down the barrels of three M-16 rifles. "Stand up, hands raised!"

The woman on the cell phone, a literal second away from saving an innocent man's life, was now defending her own against those trained to keep order and nothing else. They were in no way prepared for what the next minute would bring (after all, they were officers, not soldiers, and their guns were not quite big enough…)

"He's hurt! We need to get him to a –"

"Ma'am, you are under arrest for –"

The woman put her phone down and stood up, walking toward the officers with hands raised, still pleading for justice – for life: "Please! This man needs help! I'm a nurse, I can get him into a hospital in a second! Just let me get him to -"

But they were without reason or ration. "Ma'am, we ordered you to freeze!" the officer barked once more. "Do not get any closer or we will be forced to fire!"

"Please, just –" she took another step forward, and then another before the bullets began to explode through her chest as she fell mid-step, enough force behind the fire to blow her clear off of her feet. She flew through the air in a hail of blood and landed on her back, the first to fall but miles away from the last.

It was code for the officers from this moment on, as they were trained to eliminate those contaminated who did not follow orders (though they were also trained to affiliate themselves with bloodshed, so they took it upon themselves to keep their soiled fingers pressed firmly upon those triggers). It was a few seconds of personal Armageddon, a brief moment in which the Apocalypse set its fire as the bodies of the onlookers began to fall one-by-one, shot down in the wake of bloodlust and greed.

And yet not a soul tried to run; not a finger flinched; it was so deeply embedded within them to trust their government's judgment that it never once occurred to them that the act might be wrong. The hands behind the guns were too busy doing what they could, rather than questioning if they should. This would lead them toward their downfall (and more blood would be shed this clear-skied morning).

Within seconds it was over. The chaos fell still,

silently bestowed upon a mini-battleground, laid waste to a street full of the dead and the dying. The innocent had been raped of their justice. But this was a firefight that did not end the way the officers intended it to, because they were never trained in the event that the gun might be pointed at them (after all, who would dare question the "All-Knowing" and the "All-Seeing"?).Other than the three standing officers, there were two survivors. One was about to tell the nation how he felt with the sound of a gunshot. The other would be the only living witness as to what really took place that morning; it would be the final push upon tired shoulders.

Both were crouched behind a single dumpster, but only one was smart enough to stay, because you see, our Apocalypse is not over...

CLICK

"Move a muscle and I'll blow your fucking head off – I swear I'll do it!" With the cock of a gun, one of the officers found himself standing in death's way, with a loaded pistol pressed firmly against the temple of judgment and clarity, the beholder of "justice".

The other two officers, unprepared and suddenly instinctive in their actions (there's no code for "holy shit"), turned to face the sight before them: their fellow man of badge with this beast, this frenzied creature without a purpose (or maybe just the first to stand up for what was his), standing behind him, one hand around the officer's neck and the other holding a loaded pistol square against his temple.

"I swear I'll do it!" he screamed once more.

The other two officers raised their weapons, but at this point, neither had a clue as to what to do with them.

One stuttered:

"Drop your weapon! I won't hesitate to fire!"

The man's response was one of frenzy: "You think I'm shitting you?! I'm gonna blow this fucker's head off -
"

It was a slow-motion climax to a vicious gunfight as two automatic rifles unloaded on both their fellow comrade and this "threat to order" – this quadruped – who stood behind him, hoping that their reaction to the situation would be rewarded by ignorant minds (how would anyone know what happened?) But with due vigilance, though thoroughly misunderstood and disregarded far too often, will never collapse alone. The officer's body dropped, exposing the other man's chest, and as it began to explode with blood as the bullets punctured flesh and shattered ribs, his pistol found its line of fire square upon one of the standing officers' legs; two bullets punctured the officer's thigh, and he collapsed in a dead heap with a scream of agony.

As the last man standing dropped his M-16 and ran to his comrade's aide, it couldn't have been more ironic that the man who ordered the slaughtering of an entire street of individuals would be the one left alone and shouting for help...

*   *   *

"Someone get some help, now!" the remaining officer barked, crouched beside his fallen comrade, hoping someone would answer his pleas upon this lifeless street, littered with the bodies of the innocence he had overlooked because his orders had told him to see differently. No response. There was one: Daniel Sathers, the only remaining witness, hunched behind a dumpster, and the other (living) son of the renowned

Admiral Sathers, whose whereabouts were, at present, unknown. He could feel the sickness within him, and hence, he refused to respond, just as the Sick were trained.

"HELP!" screamed the officer (rather, screeched). Then someone appeared in a nearby doorway: a little girl, her eyes wide with innocence as she scanned the street, taking in the dead bodies like it were nothing but roadside litter. She was dressed in blue pajamas. The gunfire must have woken her up (though you would expect people to have grown used to a war zone, played out upon the streets they walk each and every day). The officer noticed her, standing in the middle of the street, amongst a sea of death.

He called out in desperation.

"Little girl! Go get help, NOW!" But the girl merely stood there, stagnant and unquestioning, staring from afar at the frazzled officer. He repeated: "GET HELP!" And the Sickness was bleeding through now, making its way within the officer, sinking beneath his skin as he felt the weight of his dying comrade upon his shoulders. "GET HELP!" She did not flinch; she did not move...just as the Sick were trained.

And then it took over. A pistol flew from his pocket,

and it cocked, the muzzle falling square upon the little girl – by far the most innocent of them all - drawn out of her home in curiosity, now staring down the barrel of a heated firearm. And yet, she could only stare - had guns lost all impact on the adrenal gland, that even a child would show no fear and no reaction to a gun aimed upon her skull?

The officer could feel the Sickness growing deeper, seeping into his bloodstream, corroding his arteries. The sweat was flowing, dispensing onto the hot concrete below, his heart racing, pounding into his ears. It overwhelmed him, fogging his thoughts. And then the situation took a turn for the worse, as a middle-aged woman intervened; she appeared in the doorway and made her way over to her daughter. "Come inside, sweetie..." when maternal instinct gave way and almost too suddenly, she could sense the presence of danger.

With a glance, she whispered: "Oh my God..."

"GET HELP!" the officer screamed, trembling with fear. His gun, once an extension of his own body, now shook in his hands, feeling like a separate entity. The mother grabbed her daughter, quiet in her actions as she made one final attempt at saving her daughter's life, but the Sickness had already bled its way through the officer's skin and into his heart.

So he pulled the trigger. The mother and her daughter, still embracing each other as they choked upon their final breaths, fell into the arms of the cold blood before them. And it was then that justice was no longer justice. Not a soul would ever question the authority of an on-call TRITE officer, nor would anyone dare challenge the hand that holds tight onto a loaded pistol...but this morning was too much; it had gone too far.

Daniel, still sitting hunched behind his source of cover (a lone dumpster), was the only one remaining within a five-mile radius that had yet to commit a homicidal act that morning, and he intended for it to stay that way, but upon the spilt blood of a child (above all, one who had, in no way, committed a crime worth being shot over), something else was slowly rising up inside of him.

The Fear did not dissipate; it exaggerated itself, until it no longer operated as a Sickness. It amplified itself upon this torso-ridden, blood-stained avenue as the screams inside slowly filled his lungs...

...until he could no longer restrain them.

The officer had no time to look, let alone react, as a savage war cry reached his eardrums. A once-unarmed

Daniel now held a tiny handgun – the same handgun previously used to shoot the downed officer (soon-to-be TWO) – and with one single breath, he aligned the shot, and he pulled the trigger until the chamber clicked empty. The officer fell, but Daniel's rage was prehistoric instinct; it was an amygdaline overdose of adrenaline. This was something primal, and it flowed through his arm and into that gun, out of spite, to show the world he wasn't done with the violence he had been holding in for so long.

He made his way over to the downed officer, raising the pistol and bringing it down upon his face, again and again, splicing his forehead open, and clearly dislocating his jaw. The scream never left his throat as he reeked vengeance upon his enemy – the government's tyranny. He then made his way over to the downed officer – the one shot in the leg, now unconscious - grabbed for his polished M-16, and fired a stern bullet through his eye.

And then it was over. Two TRITE officers was gunned down in an act of rebellion, revolution...the final breath from which the Cure was bred had cleared its lungs, and a new breed had begun. The war was on.

*   *   *

And Daniel never looked back upon a graveyard of the unburied - the decaying bodies of the Sick and the Dying, raped of their justice under gunpoint indoctrination - as he made his way past empty street junctions and curious spectators, gradually making their way toward the heart of their beloved city where the Sickness (now more feared than ever) took the lives of twenty-seven.

And as people rushed toward the crime scene, Daniel rushed away, a cocked-and-loaded pistol still in his hands. His shirt was torn and stained in blood – not his own – and his face covered in dust and ash. He had no idea where he was going, and even less understanding as to "why", but his actions and his thoughts were no longer within his control; his brain had activated the survival instinct. He was Sick, and the Sick are never Sick for very long. He ran through crowds of prying eyes for what seemed like miles, until his supply of adrenaline began to deplete, and his breath began to choke its way out of him.

He had to stop; he had to rest. Luckily, by now the crowds had dissipated; the world had found its way into the midst of the dead and rotting. Curiosity would keep Daniel alive for, at the very least, long enough to catch his breath. He stumbled away from the open street and made his way down a narrowing alleyway until finally he found himself concealed within the shadows of a decrepit city.

He sank to his knees, his back to the rest of the world, as he struggled to slow his incessant breathing. He could feel the Sickness pulsing through his veins; the Disease was alive in him. And as the sound of the screaming sirens faded into the distance, Daniel's mind raced faster and faster with every passing second.

"All those people..." He could hear them screaming for their lives. "They did nothing wrong..." The little girl fell to her knees and Daniel watched as the bullets pierced her skin. The screams began to ascend from his mind and echoed deep within his ears. He could hear her screaming as her body was consumed within the darkness of this gaping, bleeding excuse for a society. "Murder..."

And as the corpse hit the floor, a realization fell upon him, sucking him deeper into his own cesspool of thoughts. "Murder..." He knew.

"It was MURDER!"

CHAPTER FOUR

Fear can make a grown man, and a newborn infant

react precisely the same way when triggered correctly. And it was within the foundation of this most primal of human instinct that TRITE found their means of control. The being's first moments on earth will teach the same two reactions that will ultimately be felt during their last.

Fear is merely the second half of the adrenaline: "fight-or-flight" reaction. They found control by maintaining the "flight" so they would, in turn, eliminate its brother: "fight". They took precaution after precaution in order to keep basic human reaction under control so a stable environment would form, grow, and bond.

Society became crime-free; order was kept. Their plan seemed to have worked. It was order kept in check by eliminating our two basic adrenaline responses: quite possibly two of the most destructive (and productive) responses this world will ever see.

But because adrenaline is typically the response the human body receives when threatened by danger, it is meant to run free; if it is suppressed, or controlled, or contained, it will not work effectively, and in a lot of cases, leave you for dead. It was instilled within our blood in order to keep us alive, and when you take that away, or when you attempt to control it, you may see your order and control for a said amount of time, but nature has a trick up its sleeve to prevent its gifts from losing their survival instincts: the ability to break free from control, and run in its own direction, regardless of who or what it hurts when something stands in its way...

And Daniel was living proof of that, because one day, just as nature intended, someone broke free. And it takes but a single voice to start a revolution...

*   *   *

Daniel found himself crawling through wall after wall of corn stacks; a trail of blood followed with every footstep as he made his way through a shattered and forgotten field. It was not even his own blood. No more than ten minutes prior, he had been scoped out by a local butcher. Covered in the blood of a stranger, running through crowds of meddling eyes and curious faces, it was obvious that he was no longer within his own control; he was Sick.

A phone call was made, leaving Daniel with less than a two-minute window before another consignment of

TRITE officers made their way into the outskirts of the city. He was a Federal Offender now. Ducking through shadowed alleyways and hurdling dumpsters, crates, and everything the world had to offer seemed to have thrown itself into his wake, and before he knew it he found himself being chased into what had become known as the Forbidden Land – past the city's borders and into a world not many knew even existed. He had no choice; it was either death from without, or persecution from within.

It was in the sanctity of that border's passage that allowed him to properly execute his escape: TRITE Officials, regardless of the situation, were required by law to possess a warrant if they intended to cross city borders. They were protectors of the city; Daniel was property of the Outside World now.

After what seemed a lifetime of senseless, gratuitous wandering through a field of birthing corn and depths of abandoned, shattered concrete, Daniel stopped to rest; his legs could take no more of his actions (he was in no way accustomed to this sort of running – not many were).

He crawled onto his back; he felt the Sickness slowly withdrawing from his bloodstream, though his flesh remained soaked in sweat and flushed with fear and trepidation. He knew that stopping to rest was not an option right now. It takes an hour, maybe two in order to attain a warrant to leave the city, and they would be looking for him. He had witnessed the birth of a revolution; someone had fought back. After all, TRITE would do anything within their power to keep it above the ears and the eyes of a closed society.

He gathered his strength, took a breath, and pulled himself onto his feet. He began to run – to where, he had no idea. All he knew was: he needed to get away from wherever he was.

And fast.

*   *   *

Lieutenant Jameson: Co-Coordinator of the TRITE Foundation, sat in his office, staring through a window that overlooked the city, a cigarette in his mouth and a bottle of Scotch in his left hand. His right hand held a cell phone; he was awaiting a call from the head of his search team. They were in the process of obtaining the warrant to search the Forbidden Lands. He had a bad feeling about it. He took a sip of Scotch and inhaled from his cigarette, then sighed. He mumbled to himself...

"This will not end well."

His cell phone rang, and he answered without hesitation. "Yes? Yes, good. Do what you must. Find him and kill him." And with that he hung up, turning back to face his window, watching the sun as it slipped beneath the horizon. He smiled as his eyes looked out upon the land beyond the city's boundaries.

"You'll be dead before sunrise, kid..."

CHAPTER FIVE

The spotlights, glaring down in a brilliant shard of white and red, seemed no longer the problem at hand, as suddenly bullet shells were raining down upon the corn field as Daniel rushed past stalk after stalk; they exploded around him as the bullets punctured their shells and splattered the yellow seeds sharply against his flesh. In vain of what was known to them as mere "customary warnings", the TRITE officials simply held their stances within their choppers' protection as they fired blindly into the field, sightless and completely unknowing of where their target may be, yet with very little regard to maintaining a stable environment. This time they were ordered to kill, not to control their target.

And as fate would have it, it took but one misplaced footstep to send Daniel stumbling face-first into a patch of overgrowth. He rolled with his weight and suddenly he found himself facing upward, lying upon his back; he stared into a dark night's sky as suddenly, the strobe light he had been running from found its way upon him. He jumped to his feet and began to run once again, the bitter dirt hailing around him as bullets followed in his tracks. But he was too winded; he was barely able to put one foot in front of the other, let alone get them to pick up pace.

Perhaps it was his time; he was Sick, "and the Sick are never Sick for very long". As he lost his balance and fell to the floor once more, he found the Sickness consuming his veins once again. But something must have gone terribly wrong up above, as the strobe light faded and Daniel's adversary – the opposition and the coalition, antagonist and defeatist - turned around and suddenly the air fell quiet once again. Daniel mumbled: "When TRITE Officials stop and turn around, it is not hard to figure out that something has gone terribly wrong."

*   *   *

"Hold him down!" one screamed as others raced around the confinements of this sudden darkness, these walls of claustrophobic mayhem. The air was thinning as five befuddled soldiers dropped their rifles and looked around for something, anything, to hold this man down. But before anything could be done, the lone officer jerked free of one's grasp, violently pushing him to the floor before rolling back onto his feet.

"Help me! It's – it's growing stronger!" He paced his imprisonment like a madman as the others could only watch in disbelief, stunned and staring with panicked eyes. He began to claw at the metal against the side of the helicopter's interior. "You need to LET ME OFF! LET ME OFF! God help -"

And before the words could form a sentence, his head seemed to detonate with the pull of a trigger; the soldier sunk to his knees before falling over in a heap upon the metal floor below. The others turned to face the assailant, who lowered his firearm and glared at the others with disappointment, as if he had known something he should have mentioned earlier.

And he did. "I forgot to mention: Robertson is afraid of heights; the Sickness took him over," he turned to the pilot, gazing back at the situation at hand. "Turn around. We have a contaminated vessel, and it will spread to the others..."

*   *   *

Suddenly Daniel was free; both choppers turned around and returned to the city, the lights dissipating as the sound of both propellers faded into the distance, replacing a deafening silence in its wake. He knew of no reason why, and he had no intention of questioning it.

But he did have one thing to question, as he slowed his pace and felt the corn field coming to an end. Daniel found it something to keep in mind, something that should not be forgotten.

He studied his situation with lucidity, and his mind slowly wandered as he felt the Sickness pounding through his arteries and oxidizing his veins. It was within the darkest of realizations, as Daniel asked himself silently what this Sickness truly was, that finally forced him to the ground, and he found himself sitting quietly within a desolate cesspool of thoughts and questions. He disregarded the fact that he might be discovered; he disregarded the fact that he was now a Federal Offender. All he knew now was how simple it all seemed to be, yet how very complicated it truly was.

A paradigm, a tourniquet, this was beginning to grow very "Hitchcock" to him. His world was turned around. All of a sudden, he was no longer Diseased; he was no longer something to be afraid of. His adrenaline was still flowing; his Sickness was still pumping through his veins and his heart. And suddenly he found himself lost in his thoughts, and one thought in particular seemed to suck him into a darkness he had almost forgotten within the chaos of the matters at hand.

"That poor girl..."

His mind wandered until he was blind to the world around him; all he could see now was a memory he would not soon forget: the murdering of an innocent child and a mother, twenty-seven members of a society he suddenly felt obligated to protect, and all of it was over something so very human: fear. And once again his mind wandered. This time, it left its confinements, beneath a society's imprisonment, and he fell into a world he was not familiar with.

He was angry, and yet it was a Disease to thousands of men and women within the confinements of the walls of New Manhattan, he now sat on the Outskirts. The anger grew until it was odium, with teeth bared, adrenaline coursing...he was Sick as one could get, but for the first time in his life, he felt no need to restrain it...

*   *   *

"Sir, we have a downed chopper; it was Infected."

Jameson sighed and leaned his body weight against his desk. "Did we find him?"

The official was clearly intimidated, but he restrained himself. The last thing he needed was to end up like his infected comrade. "No, sir...we do know he is located somewhere within the Forbidden Lands, but we are not sure how far he has made it."

Jameson stood up and walked past the official, of whom never left his stance. A chest was opened at the back end of the office, and the sound of a gun being cocked was enough to get the Sickness flowing; he was trained to hide it well. Jameson closed the chest and secretly placed something beneath his belt.

He turned to the official. "I'll find the fucker myself."

CHAPTER SIX

The choppers were washed down as an investigation into the bombing of 87th street commenced. Something did not seem right, and people were beginning to question their safety. As always, TRITE responded with urgency. What they found was more than unsettling

(and among a sea of corpses, all being washed down in an effort to prevent contamination from spreading, how could anything be more unsettling than that and that alone?)

"Holy shit, this plate has a Presidential Sticker on it..." murmured the investigator, holding in his hands a charred and smoldering tail plate, marked with an authentic "TRITE" sticker, with the title: "President".

As the investigator turned, a blade was swung from within the darkness, spilling warm blood across the plate. The corpse fell with the rest, as the hooded man turned and fired round after round upon the remaining team of ten. In an instance, it was all over.

The man's ear hissed. "Donnie, if you aren't running by now, I'd get going...you do realize you left one alive, and he's currently making his way through Forbidden Land. Clean up the mess, call it a mystery, and get the fuck out of my city!"

Donnie removed the earpiece and thrust it to the ground next to the downed investigator. He picked up the Presidential Plate, doused the area in gasoline, and lit a match. Walking with his back to a scene of arson, he elbowed a car window, opening the door from within. He climbed in and sped off pragmatically.

*   *   *

Daniel meandered through a murky field. Locating an oddly-formatted dirt path that seemed to appear from nowhere, he decided it would be best to follow alongside, held captive by the corn maize, preventing him from being seen. He wondered where this path led, and even more so: why it began miles away from The Wall, seemingly appearing from nothingness. It was almost as if this path was not meant to lead out of the city, but rather, a road that led in suspect of another world.

Having been schooled years after The Degeneration, he was taught that there were other societies out there, but where, the textbooks never foretold. As far as he even knew, this path led to one of those societies, and perhaps they were not governed by the strap of the TRITE establishment; perhaps they were of peace.

Then again, the textbooks claimed The Wall was there for a simple reason: to prevent those other societies from getting in, and duly noted, their society was also claimed to be bound by peace, despite the lies, the bullshit, and the torrent of bloodshed witnessed daily.

His thirst was beginning to rouse, and he needed to find a source of water, and food, or he would find himself face down in this field, far too dead for TRITE's concern. Then again, was their mission to hold him captive, or to douse him in gasoline and call it a day?

He stumbled on for another hour or so before the pains in his stomach began to erupt, and he fell still. Passed out in a torrent of corn, his vision began to fade, and he lost his sense of consciousness. He began to hallucinate, seeing the little girl once more. He called out to her, screaming for her to move, but his words were dulled by the sound of a truck approaching...

*   *   *

"Where was he last seen?" Jameson whispered to his colleague, on his way to address the people of the city on the sudden disappearance of Admiral Sathers, and the new order that would now bestow due to his absence.

"Mile 9 was where they lost him, sir," the man spoke,

as the two made their way toward the podium, where a Presidential Address was to take place.

Cameras surrounded the stage that had been set up, with black and white streamers marked with the TRITE insignia: a black eagle, holding a rose in its mouth, and a grenade in its right claw, representing the turn of the world as all once knew it.

"We'll head to Mile 30 after the address. Have guards at the ready on Mile 37. He's most likely following the Path to the Enlightened...God help us if he reaches them before we do."

And with that, the official turned around, letting the new President of the TRITE Foundation send his word to the people, no matter how fabricated the disappearance of Sathers may have been. With cameras at the ready, Jameson waited patiently for his cue to speak - when every camera was thoroughly situated on him, and the new Presidential Sticker that shone upon his chest.

"It has come to our attention that Admiral Sathers is no longer an operating party member. The incident on 87th Street is obviously on the minds of the people of this city, and it must be made clear that Sathers was the first on the scene."

Jameson glanced around, a silent moment of interlude. He smiled to himself. In his head, the thoughts echoed: "They're eating this bullshit up". He then began to spew nonsense about a nonsensical situation.

"We are all aware that the situation was not contained; the Sickness was among the people of a nation I expected much more of. When the Sick are well aware that they are Sick, they are expected to remain in their homes, or shops, or businesses, or cars! It was the people of this nation that Infected Sathers, and because of said Sickness, he was under sanction of Plaguta Armada, and we were forced to put him to rest..." Jameson turned. "That is all."

CHAPTER SEVEN

Daniel awoke to his own reflection; it stared back.

"Here, drink this," a voice to his left broke the silence. Caught off-guard and at the mercy of a sudden fear that swept across him like a ghost amidst the fog, haunting and valiant, he managed the strength to turn his head.

To his side, there was a man, maybe in his mid-thirties, wearing sunglasses despite night having fallen, and vesting a tattered white shirt stained in blood (just like Daniel's), with a bottle of water in an outstretched hand. Daniel jumped from his seat, hitting his head on the roof of the vehicle he was now bound to.

"Where am I? Who are you?!"

"Relax, kid, you're in safer hands than you were back there. At least in the present situation." The man thrust the bottle of water into Daniel's forefront. "Drink!"

Daniel took the bottle of water, removed the cap, and began to gulp until nothing remained. The man offered a second bottle, and Daniel chugged it down without reluctance. Satiated, he glanced down, noticing a pistol in the man's lap, and a TRITE insignia tattooed on his right forearm.

"You're one of them..." Daniel jumped once more. The man removed his sunglasses, revealing a foggy left eye, clearly blind and without sight. He stopped the vehicle, next to a sand-embalmed sign reading: "Mile 18".

"I was one of them..."

Without words, Daniel glanced once more at the pistol. "Well, why are you –"

"We have a lot in common, Daniel..." the man spoke

as the vehicle began to move once more, the world around it now ricocheting and cascading its way upon the reflective surface of a tinted window. Daniel stared deep through its confinement as the man erratically explained his paramount.

"I saw you when I was in that window..."

The detonator was pushed, and the tow truck exploded.

"When everyone else rushed to the scene of the crime, you rushed away, crouching behind a dumpster like a frightened dog with its tail between its legs..."

People raced to the scene, trying to pull Sathers from the vehicle, as Daniel crouched behind the dumpster... "Then TRITE showed up, which was planned; Jameson and I expected it...we counted on it..."

"Wait, Lieutenant Jameson?"

Donnie turned to face Daniel.

"...Yes, the esteemed."

Jameson placed the detonator in Donnie's hand...

"He threatened me with death, if I were to say

'no'...what would you have done? You know damned well what TRITE has the power to do – you, of all people, can understand, correct?"

"So you killed –"

"Sathers? Yes..."

"But who will take his place?"

Donnie stopped the car once more. He turned to face a nervous Daniel, replacing his sunglasses. He glared through them. "The snake that put the detonator in my hand, Daniel."

*   *   *

Jameson boarded the chopper. This one was fresh, as the other two had been thoroughly cleansed of the blood of the Sickness, burned to mere ash. Several soldiers boarded behind him. In minutes, it took off, passing the imprisonment of The Wall, and into Forbidden Land...

*   *   *

They passed Mile 24. A walkie-talkie jettisoned from Donnie's hand, as he listened to blood-soaked words. "We'll cut him off at Mile 30." Donnie lowered the walkie-talkie. "Shit."

"What?" Daniel queried.

"They're going to try and cut us off at Mile 30," Donnie sparred as he cocked the weapon in his lap. "Though I could have expected this – why do you think I brought the damned gun?"

"Yeah, because a shoot-out is exactly what I call a rescue mission", Daniel reached to the back seat for another bottle of water. It was then that he fingered a cold muzzle. "Shit!"

Donnie turned. "I never said that this was a Rescue Mission, you arrogant dick!"

"I'm not sharing any part of this! It's bad enough I'm sitting in a car with a blind TRITE –"

Donnie stopped the car. He turned to face Daniel.

"You do realize what this is, Daniel? Huh?! DO YOU?!" And suddenly the motive here was clear: Daniel was not being rescued; he was not being saved.

He was a hostage, as Donnie's cold, steel muzzle pressed firm against his temple. "This is my celebration! My inauguration from a TRITE menace! Do you have any idea what TRITE has done to me, Daniel?! My family?! My friends?! They've used them – as pawns, tourniquets – in an unforgiving game of foxhunt!"

*   *   *

Jameson's chopper landed at Mile 30.

"Set up here. Show no mercy. We're in Forbidden Land. What happens here, should remain closed in its casket walls..."

*   *   *

"I'm sorry –" Daniel began.

"Sorry won't bring them back!" Donnie dragged the gun from Daniel's neck and sighed loudly. He could feel the Sickness in his throat, in his heart.

"I'm sorry, Daniel...the Sickness has not bared this flesh for some time. I forgot how it felt..."

Daniel combed his neck with his hand. "It's okay."

Donnie began moving the car forward once more. "Do you know what the Sickness is, Daniel? It's a makeshift; a lie. It's an emotion as common to the human body as you are to this land beyond the Wall. It's fear; it's anger; it's everything."

Daniel twitched. "We were told –"

"It's not about what you were told. It's about what they neglected to tell you. You were born with an adrenal gland. Why would you birth with something you weren't meant to use?"

Daniel thought about it, which seemed to be more of the problem than the solution. Having to think about a question as estranged as that was near abysmal. Donnie stared him down.

"You actually have to think about it?" Donnie knew that there was perhaps only one way to show Daniel. He picked up pace, pressing his foot harder upon the gas pedal. "You feel that?"

The bumps in the road were masked as Daniel could no longer feel the vehicle jettisoning around like a plane shot down in flight. It was now his heart that was thrusting, faster and faster, the adrenaline masking his thoughts. "Please, slow down..."

"NO! You feel that, Daniel?! That gut-wrenching terror in your throat? That feeling in your stomach, telling you to slow down? That's instinct, Daniel! Embrace it!"

It was then that the car sped past Mile 29, and Donnie caught the sign's frame out of the corner of his good eye. Daniel, too consumed within the Sickness, alive in his stomach, gashing through his skin, beneath his flesh, in his veins...never saw the bullets coming as they rained down upon the car's frame...

CHAPTER EIGHT

"See that?" Jameson cocked his gun as the car buckled, bullets ricocheting off of its steel frame. "That's a terrorist caught in the midst of his own reflection..." Jameson ordered onto his walkie-talkie: "Take them both out!"

*   *   *

Daniel could feel his heart in his throat, bursting with a blood-coddling stimulus. "What the fuck is that?!"

Donnie reached for his gun. "That's the sound of wolves." He placed a pistol in Daniel's hand.

"You obviously know how to use one of these...? I saw you use one once before..." Daniel caressed the cold, burdening steel with his finger. "You want me to shoot them?!" When suddenly, Donnie hit a small button on the side of his window.

Daniel's seat began to retract backward without his control. "I want you to shoot me if this vehicle is stopped," Donnie said as he seized hold of an M-16 with a TRITE insignia on its muzzle. "For the time being..."

Donnie shot the M-16 against Daniel's door; it tattered from its locus and flew off, leaving Daniel in the line of fire.

*　　　　*　　　　*

As the truck approached, TRITE was ordered to stop firing. Jameson approached the vehicle, as it began to slow, when suddenly the passenger's seat door flew from its pose. Cocking his weapon, Jameson stood in front of the vehicle, still moving. "200 miles per hour and in the wrong fucking lane."

He smiled, and ranged his weapon...

*　　　　*　　　　*

Donnie aimed his own. He growled: "Jameson..." And as former Lieutenant Jameson approached the vehicle, his gun aimed square against Donnie's head, he pressed upon the gas once more, leaving Jameson with two options: move the fuck out of the way, or become yet another dead TRITE officer.

"Daniel..." But Daniel was consumed in the grasp of

the Sickness, clutching onto his chest with a clenched fist. "Fuck it." Donnie aimed the M-16 against the windshield and fired. The glass rained down upon Daniel as bullets thrust through the bodies of several dozen TRITE officers, now suddenly thrown into the midst of a chaos they created upon this barren, lifeless land. "I'm sorry, Daniel. We're almost there..."

*   *   *

"Donnie! You son of a bitch!" Jameson cocked his gun and shot three rounds before jumping out of the way, as the vehicle careened past him at 80 miles per hour.

"Shoot this fucker!" But it was too late; the vehicle had passed. TRITE rushed to their vehicles, leaving a soot-faced Jameson alone, screaming: "Shoot him!" But in the grip of the very fear they were supposed to monitor, they had ducked their way behind cover, as an M-16 unloaded shells from the careening vehicle.

*   *   *

"Put pressure on it!" Donnie screamed at Daniel, but the blood was now gushing onto the seat below at too rapid a pace for simple pressure to attend to it. Daniel, frenzied, dropped his gun and held tightly onto the bullet wound, ensued from his (and Donnie's), nemesis: a gawking Admiral Jameson.

"What...what do I...?" and it was then that a pained Daniel slipped from consciousness. Donnie, not knowing what to do, could only keep going, faster and faster...

*   *   *

Daniel awoke to a shattered valley: trees splintered, a bridge in the distance torn from the brink of a cliff, and cars...but they were unmoving, silent. Looking around, it was daytime; the sun was now shimmying off of a nearby lake, almost mocking his presence with a red overcast (with due note: the lake was dried up, but it seemed to have maintained enough moisture to glisten lightly with the red horizon). To his right, a skyscraper stood sound, the base crippled, with concrete splintering the asphalt below.

"Can you hear me, Daniel?" a voice to his left.

Daniel responded: "Where are we?"

Donnie appeared, with another: a man in a gray suit. He lowered himself to Daniel's level, gazing upon him. "This one has seen some war!" Looking down, Daniel noticed his bullet wound had been tended to: a hole in his jeans, the wound was stitched and brazened with cotton gauze.

"Who are you –?"

"The question is not: who am I. The question is: who the hell are you and what are you doing here?" It was then that Daniel noticed the man brandished a silver firearm, compelled confidently against Donnie's head. Several others were emerging from the tree line, guns aimed at them.

Donnie tried to answer. "Well, we're here for your protection-" but he was cut off as the man lifted Donnie's sleeve, revealing the TRITE insignia.

"You're one of them...?"

Daniel tried to stand, but he was slowly escorted back to the ground by someone behind him. In this moment of chaos, Daniel wondered silently: "Where the fuck am I...?" as Donnie spoke with the man in gray.

"We are Runners, like you," Donnie explained. "Do you think we just wandered out of TRITE's valiance to have you fix my friend's leg up? We were shot at –"

"I know you were shot at, Mister...Donnie, is it? We watched from our skyscraper as several TRITE ensembles fired upon your vehicle; we watched and wondered: 'What on God's once-green earth are these fuckers doing?!'"

"We were running. Sathers is dead...and this is his son." It was then that the man in gray looked upon Daniel with shallow eyes. He turned to Donnie.

"You neglected to tell me this was the son of Admiral Sathers." The man in gray turned to stare down at Daniel's weary body.

He held out a hand and Daniel hesitantly clasped onto it and was then pulled up by the burly Runner. Daniel knew these men – not by name, but as

"Runners"; his father had spoken of them many times...

*   *   *

"Daniel, I want you to remember these words: those outside of this Wall are there because they were plagued once. They are called 'Runners'; they are men who have escaped the Wall, too Sick to know where they are going, and they reside there for just that purpose", Sathers spoke to Daniel as a young boy.

"You need to worry less about what's outside of that Wall and more about the nuisance within it. We are at war with a Disease far too exemplified than you can imagine. I want you to promise me, you will never leave this Wall! You will never seek the aide of the Runners, for they will kill you without sympathy..."

*   *   *

The man in gray smiled. "Pardon our dust, Mister Sathers, but we have been sought out by TRITE many times. You understand our predicament. We are here to help those like us...but you most certainly are not like us." He raised the gun to Donnie's head. "Shit, Sathers, you're more 'TRITE' than this son-of-a-bitch!" He turned to one of his comrades. "Tell me why I haven't shot this fucker dead yet?" He cocked the pistol. "TELL ME!"

He then signed, almost exhausted by his own presence, like a poltergeist tired from a night's weary haunting. "Daniel, what would you say to this: you can stay here, but by noon tomorrow you are gone – both of you. If not, I shoot your TRITE-branded friend through the temple, and then use you as a hostage. You're worth a lot of money, Daniel...don't make me shoot this fucker."

"Okay, okay!" Daniel pushed the gun away. The man lowered his weapon. Again, he extended a hand toward Daniel, this time to shake it.

"My name is Raul. I was banished here...it seems TRITE does not take kindly to other races and ethnicities. They were going to Cleanse me using that mind-fuck they call the Manhattan Square Vaccination, but I refused."

Daniel shook the hand gratefully. They began to walk toward the skyscraper to the right, a good forty stories high, and very palpable to the naked eye. Raul continued, as his crew of gun-wielding acquaintances followed, scoping the abandoned street with the eyes of paranoid tempers and deviated consciousness.

"They wanted to use me as a pawn to show the people of New Manhattan that intolerance of the rules they provide bring more than the peace of death...so they sent me – stripped naked and branded –" He lifted up his right sleeve, revealing a TRITE insignia, just like Donnie's. "...and left me to die out here."

"Why do they not tolerate your race?" Daniel inquired.

"Because your father was of Nazi descent," Donnie spoke from behind. The group laughed, but Donnie did not; Donnie never laughed (TRITE did not tolerate humor, or anything, when put into that context).

Daniel wiped his brow; he could not defend such a statement. His father was of Nazi descent, though not many knew that, nor did they know what a Nazi even was. Raul smiled.

"Come...I'll show you what you've missed."

CHAPTER NINE

"Damnit, damnit, damnit!" Jameson sat in his office once again, watching the news as the people of a pragmatic nation began to riot in the streets.

"Sathers' disappearance has left many questioning their safety," spoke the news reporter. "I stand here at New Times Square, as protestors riot about the new government-issued changes..." Behind her, several men and women with picket signs paced the streets, reading:

"Freedom is free from reason..."

"My job, my life, my time..."

"We are the 99 percent..."

Jameson turned the television off. Turning to one of his disciples, he muttered: "Do these people not know what we're protecting them from?! It's like they have no idea what's outside of that Wall! Chaos! Upheaval! Why are they doing this?!"

"Do you think Admiral Sathers' death would go without questions?" said the disciple. Jameson turned to face him.

"There's only one way to end a protest properly, Andy, especially one among a city filled with no reason and no fear: we must drag that boy through the streets and show them what it looks like when their despicable Sickness bleeds!"

*   *   *

Raul led Daniel and Donnie toward a stairwell, where they climbed thirty-three stories before Raul unlocked one of the staircase doors and they entered. Passing through a small lobby, with a shattered desk at the front (clearly for a Receptionist of some nature), Raul began to explain what Daniel never knew...

"Did you ever wonder where TRITE came from, Daniel? And Donnie, I urge you to keep quiet; do not interrupt, because you need to know this, as well," Raul spoke solemn words.

"I was told –" Daniel began.

"You were told lies, Daniel. TRITE formed in 2021, exactly twenty years after the Twin Towers fell. It was 2011 – ten years prior – that the nation fell victim to a recession. The streets were told to have been lined with gold here; this city once held Wall Street; this city once held the Statue of Liberty; this city was once a place of great power, even more so than D.C." Raul led them toward a nearby window. He pressed his palm against the glass. He recalled Former Manhattan...

"In 2001, Sathers' first son was a New York policeman. He entered the building the moment the first plane hit the tower, and he never made it out alive. The building soon collapsed –"

Raul led them past an office suite, where chairs and tables were upturned. An old, makeshift American flag stood pompously against one of the walls. Daniel stared at the oddity.

"What flag is that?" he spoke as he approached.

"That's the American flag - before TRITE took power," Raul said as he approached. "TRITE was the ordinance behind the Twin Tower epidemic that caused a massive war – a war that never ended. As far as we know, the societies outside of here are still battling in a sea of hot sand..."

Daniel located a magazine on one of the desks as Raul spoke of the incident. The print date read: "September 13th, 2001" and on the cover stood two shattered buildings. One image displayed that of a 707 Boeing airplane, half-cruised into the building itself. The other had already collapsed.

"TRITE staged the crash..." Donnie reiterated. "Wait..." Donnie rushed to the window. He located in the distance the Manhattan Bridge, shattered beyond recognition. He then stared upon the East River, dried up and filled with dust. He then took a look around the building. "This is..."

"They rebuilt the Towers, and you're standing in one of them. The other has been gone for a long time...a long time..."

*   *   *

The white Lexus was shimmied with rain, bouncing off of the polished exterior like crickets leaping from leaf to leaf, as it sped into the midst of police cars, men in riot gear, and three dead bodies laid upon the ground, covered by a white sheet (the blood soaked through). Claus Sathers never bothered removing the key from the car ignition as he let the car park; it jerked him forward, and he hit his head on the steering wheel, but this was no time for pain intolerance, as his worst fears may lie beneath one of those blood-soaked white sheets.

Pushing his way past news reporters, he caught audio of one on the scene of the shooting: a blonde woman with a camera to her front, and the school behind her, police lights intermittent all around. "Yet another school shooting took place today at 8:01 AM, just before the students were entering the building..."

No time to listen, as Sathers made his way over to the yellow police tape, before suddenly an officer stopped him.

"I think that's my son!" Sathers yelled in panic.

"This is an evidentiary location, sir. If it's your son, you'll know once we know, okay?" the officer said. Sathers made one last attempt to push past him, but two others appeared – bulky brethren of a bleeding society – and forced him on his way. "Keep moving!"

And then Sathers was just another face among the crowd that had gathered. All he could do was listen to the report: "We have no word on the victims' names yet, but the shooter was not even a member of this school. Shooting one security guard through the head, and then unloading round after round upon the teens that were mere feet from the building's entrance, his motive is speculative. An eyewitness reported that he yelled: 'This is for the fear this nation has brought upon us', right before pulling the trigger on himself..."

*				*				*

Jameson sat in an office once again, puffing on a Cuban cigar (the nation itself had vanished in the torrent of The Great Degeneration; he had paid $10,000 for it years prior, hoping it would be smoked on a day of victory - oh, how wrong he was). He stared at what was Admiral Sathers' office. It was much bigger, and the walls were lined with newspaper clippings, photos and posters of campaigns he had run and awards he had won...

"Sathers ends The Great Degeneration..."

"Sathers promises to end fear for New Manhattan..."

"Sathers is interviewed on his take on the Sickness..."

Jameson stood, intrigued by the last article. He pulled it from the wall, snapping the frame that held the newspaper up, and began to comb through the words.

"The Sickness is more than just a disease or an illness. It is an epidemic. I was around before The Great Degeneration, and I saw what the Sickness did to societies, time and time again. It brings upon war; it brings upon violence; it brings upon a catatonic desire to hunt, to kill, to mate, and to repeat."

Jameson thrust the article – frame intact – against the window behind him. "Son of a bitch was out of his mind." He stood and paced toward the liquor cabinet when suddenly his phone rang. He answered without urgency: "Yes?"

On the other end: "Sir, we've found him. We've found all of them. They're at Mile 91, Junction 1. Awaiting your orders."

Jameson smiled a crooked smile. "Mile 91, Junction 1?" He laughed. "Where do you think they got the fucking name from? Load up every off-guard TRITE officer into a chopper, a plane, strip cars and strap machine guns to their fucking roofs! I don't care what you do, just pick me up at Sathers' old office and make sure no one is afraid of heights this time!" He hung up. "I've got you, you son-of-a-bitch..."

CHAPTER TEN

Raul led Daniel and Donnie into a closed-off room. "TRITE would surely lynch both of you for simply entering this chamber." He picked up a book, handing it to Daniel. The title read: "United States History, 2018" - clearly a textbook.

Blowing the dust off of the book, he began to open the specimen. Raul turned and reached over with lightning-bolt swiftness and grabbed Daniel's hand. "Don't say I didn't warn you when you get to page 217..."

Daniel tentatively opened the book to the first page; an American flag stood proudly, annunciated, waving with a slight breeze. He began to read as Donnie paced the room. "So what's so special? I just see textbooks and Stephen King novels, whoever the fuck that is. What's so damned unique or forbidden about these scriptures that would cause TRITE to 'lynch me'?"

Raul stared him down, gawking, laughing. "A member of the TRITE movement just asked me why a fucking textbook dating back before The Great Degeneration, is worth dying over. My dreams come true at last!"

Donnie leaned in closer. "What's so fucking special?"

Raul smiled, not fazed. "It's the past, that's what."

"Quiet, both of you!" Daniel yelled timidly, his eyes

never leaving the words imprinted in black ink upon a 345-page book interior. "This is everything they never answered me about in class. These books hold the past! They hold the secret to –"

"Remember, page 217, Daniel..." Raul interrupted, as he led his way out of the room. Donnie followed, making his way with Raul toward the kitchen, but Daniel was not to follow this morning. He had several dozen reading assignments to do (345 pages, actually), and he was far behind on his homework...

*   *   *

"Page 217: on January 20th, 2016, Clause Sathers was elected President of the United States, with an electoral vote far surpassing the average electoral and popular vote by almost 44 percent..." Daniel combed through the words. Night was falling, but yet he had yet to blink. Donnie had checked on him at one point, or so Daniel thought.

"Was it him or was I hallucinating?" Raul had also mentioned something about "...the two of you are going to be miles from here..." but yet again, Daniel barely listened; the world around him was a time warp, and history came alive – history he had been deprived of, satiated of – like puppets being moved along by the strings of the past, dancing between every line, between every sentence. The past 216 pages had been interesting, yes - Daniel learned about the many wars, America's infatuation with oil and the eventual collapse of the economy in 2008, leading to a worldwide slump; the war never ended, and it was then that page 217 unfolded...

"Promising to end a worldwide fear: terrorism, Sathers breezed through his first two years of Presidency with stride: he managed to end the war in Iraq; the economy recovered, slow but steady; Sathers did as promised: he ended terrorism..."

Daniel could not seem to move his eyes from the word: "terrorism". It seemed so ironic, so calculated, that his campaign was directed toward the physical form of "fear" itself, that it was almost as if yes, he ended terrorism in his time, but perhaps the meaning of the word "terror" was something far different to him. Who, exactly, were the terrorists he, as an individual, felt like combatting? It was confirmed on the next page, when suddenly, Sathers' story took a turn downhill.

"The world was at peace, but upon suffering the

death of one of his four sons during a school shooting on March 21st, 2020, the duties of the President were soon passed onto the Senate. May 21st, 2020 – three months later – an unexplained incident involving what is believed to have been a terrorist attack killed several Party Members. The survivors, over the following weeks, were slowly but surely assassinated..."

"Hey, kid!" Raul stood in front of Daniel's one source of illumination: a candle, half-melted to the base with hot wax. He glanced up, waking from a stupor.

"Yeah...?" Daniel replied, wiping his eyes with his fingertips, when suddenly it became clear that Raul brandished a loaded M-16 rifle, rusted and dingy, but perhaps functional.

"You just killed the entire camp," Raul said austerely.

Daniel stood up, when suddenly the walls shook as some sort of explosive hit one of the floors below them. Raul grabbed Daniel by the arm and pulled him toward the stairwell. Daniel lapsed for the book, and hid it in his pants' liner, covering it with his shirt; he did not want to let Raul see he was taking it, and though the risk might have been grave, it seemed Raul had a far larger issue to deal with.

They made it to the 27th floor landing before a window was within reach. Daniel had just enough time to glance upon the once-empty dirt road, now lined with TRITE vehicles, soldiers emptying from the backs while two men manned the machine gun atop each van; choppers circled the area, lighting the desert with white illumination.

"Shit!" Daniel gulped as Raul pulled him down to the bottom floor, before suddenly a familiar voice came into earshot via an electronic loud horn.

"Donnie Roberts and Daniel Sathers, please exit the sky-scraper with your hands up. If you comply, we will spare the rest of the Runners; we will not seek them; we will not pursue them. If you don't come out...well, let's just say this tower will have to fall by the hands of yet another plane..."

A jet screeched high above.

Raul turned to look upon Daniel. "Don't worry, you're not going anywhere." They approached the lobby of the building, the lights off, and darkness coating all except for a single blinding incandescence, shot from an industrial-sized floodlight, muzzled upon the bottom floor, where shadows crept like banshees as the Runners made their way slowly toward the entryway...

Donnie lowered himself below Daniel. He whispered closely, as if he wanted the others out-of-earshot: "If I know the TRITE Operation as well as I think I do, they'll be lowering onto the roof of this fucking wreck in about ten seconds."

He grabbed Daniel by the shoulder and led him through a double-doorway that ran into the lobby's kitchen. Donnie continued: "See that spot-light? It's a distraction." With a suddenness he turned, grabbing Daniel by the shoulders and staring into his eyes with the look of a man who was preparing himself for death. He paused, his voice suddenly rasping, so much so that spit spewed from his lips.

"What are you talking about?" Daniel whispered.

"The moment that spotlight is turned off, Daniel, you'll have exactly 37 seconds to get from here and to the elevator. I scoped it out when I knew TRITE was going to come looking. The shaft is empty; the elevator car isn't even there. Crawl into it – it may be a ten-foot drop but damnit, at least one of us needs to be able to say they made it through this...alive..."

And then Donnie thrust Daniel with the strength of ten thousand madmen against one of the kitchen carts, and made a slow but expedited pace toward the lobby's front doorway...

CHAPTER ELEVEN

Donnie exited the building, his hands raised, which was quite difficult, as the spotlight shone a bright luminosity. Guns raised, TRITE officers clicked their safeties off (it was soon becoming clear to Donnie that the point of TRITE having safeties on their weapons in the first place was a poor decision budget-wise). Jameson seemed to appear from nothingness and was the only one who had come dressed for the occasion.

He glanced around. "Where's the boy?"

"Turn the damned light off and I'll tell you," Donnie told Jameson, who, unknowing of the intention, nodded in the light's direction, and it slowly dwindled into darkness.

"There, the light's off. Now, the boy –"

"The 'boy' won't be joining us today, Jameson."

Jameson stared back with a solemn expression.

Donnie could only laugh. "You're as stupid as you fucking look right now," Donnie lowered his arms. "By the way, great show with the new tanks." He signposted toward one of the vans, totted with a machine gun built to its dome. "Would love to see it in action one of these-"

"Shoot him," Jameson shouted, and without question

or hesitation (TRITE had neither), they did as they were told...

*   *   *

"No, no, no!" Daniel screamed as he reached the elevator shaft. He was surprised to see that one of two things were omnipresent: either Donnie's good eye was about as functional as his bad one, or there were two different elevators - and this was not the right one. The elevator car was, very much so, intact. Hearing footsteps above, Daniel knew he had to do something; he had to tell the Runners that their guns were being pointed in the wrong direction. Though perhaps the war had already begun, as he had just heard the echoing of machine guns.

And so he rushed through the kitchen, but halfway there the floor burst open, and he was blinded by an effervescent gas. TRITE was not far behind. Not knowing what to do, Daniel lurched away from the lobby, as much as he could, as TRITE crept upon the backs of several hundred men with loaded guns and everything to die for.

Hiding within a room filled with nothing but pipes – for what reason, he did not know – he could hear TRITE as they did something incredibly stupid: they shouted before they shot, and Daniel could only assume that was not in their best of interests, as two hundred guns – not the ones Daniel was used to, as these ones sounded like they were meant to hurt, not kill – broke the sound barrier. Another two hundred guns responded; these ones were familiar.

They sounded less meant for war, less accustomed to hurting; the bullets did not ricochet but instead, they exploded. It was a good thirty seconds before the number of guns fell one-by-one, and which side was winning was a mystery to him. All he could think was: "It doesn't matter who wins right now, because either way, I'm going to die today..."

And then an explosion knocked him onto his back and pipes rained down upon him...and that seemed to trigger his life to flash before his eyes, but this was no life. How could anyone consider this atrocity, this unfortunate series of events, to be, at all, accountable as a life? First he was sheltered, shunned from asking questions and thrown dirty looks when asked: "Why can't I leave this city? What's out there?"

Then he was banished from that world, thrown into

the paradox that suddenly, his questions were answered, and he was now reminded that maybe it was better when he didn't know. And now, he was about to die, and all he wanted from the start was to be more like his father, and understand the world he lived in without having to ask the questions: "Why" or "How"?

And that was it. Only one thing left to do now...

He removed the book from his pants liner, and he turned to page 217, where his answer lay...

*   *   *

"Sathers soon disappeared, and the world fell into a cold swelter. Without a Senate to run the country during Sathers' disappearance, anarchy broke out in the streets; a deep recession hit, and many were forced from their homes. It was then that the United States was at its most vulnerable, and Germany was the first to attack; Russia soon joined the battle, and without an Army to defend a wrought nation (the Pentagon had been closed since 2018, which was by decree of the President himself), history was erased, and no one knows what happened between March 2021, and March 2023.

"Sathers soon returned to a nation that had destroyed itself from within, and it was then that Sathers eliminated contact with the outside world, and so began The Great Degeneration. The nation split into sectors: a Western and an Eastern. Contact between the two was lost, and a wall was erected around Manhattan, where he soon took upon himself a superficial power..."

Another explosion threw Daniel from his trance. TRITE had entered the building. This was it: death by firing squad. Another explosion. Then Daniel noticed the pipes. A good four-foot piece of steel, he realized that perhaps he had stumbled into the perfect place...

"Daniel, come out with your hands in the air!" the loud horn beckoned, as Daniel heard the footsteps growing closer...

He grabbed hold of one, checking its weight with his hands. It was then that a smoke grenade settled within the kitchen, and there was only one thing left to do now. Rushing the danger in a silhouette, he lurched from the small room, adrenaline flowing. He recalled his trip in the car with Donnie:

"You feel that? That's instinct! Embrace it!"

He found himself squared against a muzzle, and it was now or never. And so he swung; the M-16 flew through the air and hit the wall, discharging a few rounds before landing in a heap upon the floor. Daniel swung again; a gas mask soared from the man's head, and Daniel grabbed for it, pragmatically using it to cover his face and allowing him to maneuver around the kitchen without choking inanely on what seemed to be an amalgamation of white smoke and tear gas.

Hearing coughing to his right, he swung a third time, and the officer landed at his feet. The others, curious as to the rounds that had fired upon Daniel's mighty blow, made their way slowly through the mist. They crept toward where the gun had fired but found nothing.

"Alright, keep looking –" and it was then that Daniel emerged from the remnants of empires past due, like a Phoenix rising from the embers of an odious empire, and as guns raised, Daniel let go of his fear; he embraced his Sickness...and he pulled the trigger.

Two officers collapsed, knocking over several kitchen utility shelves. Firing into the smoke, Daniel shielded himself behind a stove. Realizing it was a gas-based appliance, he blind-fired over it, suppressing the officers long enough for him to sprint around a corner. The officers did as he expected: they fired upon the stove, and it exploded in a brilliant blaze.

By the time the fire and smoke had cleared, Daniel had already made his way around a second corner, reaching the lobby. There was nothing but death before him. Every Runner, every officer (except the few still looking for him, somewhere not far behind) laid in a bloodied heap; the walls were stained with a crimson glow as Admiral Jameson made his way toward the front door, a revolver in his right hand...

CHAPTER TWELVE

Jameson kicked in the front door, gun raised, but it was not going to be of much use tonight, as the butt of an M-16 swung from his left and bashed in his hand; the gun dropped. Darkness crept upon him as Daniel's liberation of a disease that did not exist, suddenly became very, very clear. The officers that remained must have seen much of the commotion, but fearing the potential killing of Admiral Jameson, who was far too close for comfort, they did not fire. Daniel turned and unloaded every last round in that chamber with an emotionless gesture. Then the gun in Daniel's hands dropped, and a figure appeared with but a single luminance brought on by the spotlight outside, as without orders it turned back on.

"Daniel, you're under arrest in the sanctity of –"

"Plaguta Armada, being Sick, call it whatever the fuck you want, Jameson!" Daniel welded a new weapon now, and in almost a satirical gesture, he uppercut Jameson's jaw with the very book he had stolen – the book that bared the truth (and the truth was simple: Jameson was part of a lie, and that lie was going to be his end). Jameson tried to throw a punch, but the darkness was to be Daniel's shepherd, and the swing missed. The book swung again, knocking Jameson onto the blood-soaked floor below. He turned to gaze upon the very conscious of The Sickness in the flesh: a man welding a weapon – what that weapon was, it did not matter – and set out with every possible intention on killing another, born from odium.

"Stand up," Daniel commanded, but Jameson felt it would be smarter to reach for the small handgun he kept in his right shoe. In an act of chance – almost a literal game of Russian Roulette – he fired, but through the shadows (and blurred vision, thanks to the two blows he had taken from a 400-page hard-cover textbook) the bullet missed.

Daniel was quick in his actions, for this was perhaps the first time in his life that The Sickness had a purpose; it had a meaning, and it had a name. This was what the TRITE organization – more importantly, his father – was protecting their society from. It was a feeling that truly fathomed no "good"; nothing of value or worthiness could possibly come from this emotion; it was the cause of every problem, and the burden of every solution.

This was a primal desire to see blood, and as Daniel relentlessly beat Jameson with the book (he soon grappled the gun from Jameson's dislocated hand, and beat him with that instead), all he could think of was how good this felt. It satiated an instinct that simply cannot be controlled, and though perhaps if Daniel had not left town, and if perhaps he had not become a liability to the all-knowing, all-seeing TRITE organization, their ever-so-true New Manhattan would have remained "cured".

And as Jameson finally fell into unconsciousness (note that this did not stop Daniel from swinging, and swinging, and swinging...) it dawned upon Daniel that the man scattered beneath him was the man that ordered his father's assassination, and a wave of sadness crept over his frazzled body with what could only be described as winter – a blizzard, rather. And so he stopped, placed the gun in his pocket (making sure the safety was firmly pressed inward), and left Jameson lying among two hundred dead bodies – half of whom he had sent in to perform but a simple task: find Daniel, and if it meant killing him, they would have done that, too.

Was life that meaningless?

He passed Donnie's body on the way out of the building, where abandoned TRITE vehicles smoldered, and a jet screeched off into the distance (Jameson gave the orders here, and Jameson was no longer conscious). He bent to check his pulse, but it was evident that this man was formally deceased. He had but one thing left to do now. Reaching into Donnie's pocket, he removed a set of car keys and paced toward Donnie's truck.

CHAPTER THIRTEEN

And so Daniel drove – to where, he did not know. He passed Mile 106 several hours prior, and after that, it seemed as if the signs just stopped coming; they had no purpose anymore, and for what reason, he did not know. The sun was beginning to show itself upon the brim of the horizon; dawn was coming. Driving a truck with a missing passenger's door and a shattered windshield, it would be refreshing to see some sun (Daniel had seen enough darkness for one night...)

Fifteen times Daniel thought: "Why didn't I kill him? Why didn't I shoot him through the head like he was going to do to me?" And fifteen times, Daniel's fists slammed against that steering wheel, livid like angry snakes. Sometime near Mile 200 (or what he assumed was Mile 200 – all context of space had lost presence), Daniel had also come to the realization that his father was dead.

Another angry fist, tired and taunting, curled up with rage and pummeled that steering wheel once more. He was not upset that his father was dead – the emotions were much like icebergs, Daniel culminated: the visible portion is the action from without – the part of sentiment that shows itself on the outside, usually in the form of a facial expression, or a tear. It will not destroy the boat, but it will act as a warning: stay the fuck away from it, because it is bigger than it looks.

But the dangerous part – the part that rips the hull of the boat to shreds – is below the surface; it is beneath the skin. It is the part that may not show itself; it may not bear teeth, but if you do not navigate yourself properly, you will learn the true meaning of "sunken", and perhaps that is where the term: "sunken emotion" comes from.

The truck began to slow; it was running low on Ethanol. Daniel sighed, removed his belongings (among them: the book he had stolen) from the vehicle, and began to walk – to where, he did not know. All he could think about was: how many times he had asked teachers point-blank about: "What's out there?" and their enigmatic responses: "There are other societies, but they are Sicker than you could possibly imagine". Was this said to keep people from exiting the Wall, or was this true?

Apparently he would soon find out.

*   *   *

Jameson awoke to a cold sweat. Where was he? Why was he here? He glimpsed around, and realized he was lying atop a bloodied corpse. Jumping up in shock, he fell once more; his balance was offset (it might have had to do with the dislocated jaw he now bared, or perhaps the shattered rib cage Daniel had left him with – a hell of a parting gift).

An echoing resonated from his pocket. He removed the walkie-talkie and pressed upon the dispatch button. "I'm at the old Memorial. Someone fucking come and get me – now!" He thrust with all of his might, reaching with a broken arm toward his jaw; he popped it back into place. The pain was excruciating, but pain was far from his grasp. When madness is all you know, there is plenty of time to account the repercussions of something as useless as pain. It is simply a state-of-mind.

The wait would be a good twenty minutes, so he felt the need to scope out the location. The stairwells were locked, and the elevator was a mess, so he wandered around the bottom floor, until he reached the 9-11 tribute: a gold-plated wall inscribed with the names of those who had died on September the 11th, 2001. He caressed it with a bloodied hand, feeling the etchings with shaking hands and numb fingers. "They died with purpose..."

CHAPTER FOURTEEN

The sun was rising, casting hellish contrasts upon the sand-ridden dunes he now roamed. With nowhere to go except forward, he marched on into nothingness, dry and numb. He assumed that by now, he should be sweating, but it seemed as if the heat was so strong, that the beads of tepid water never made it to the ground; they balled up into tiny constellations upon his brow and neck, disintegrating before they had a chance to drip and soak into his torn, bloodied shirt.

This was no normal heat. And then he saw it. Had he been walking in a circle? How could the sight before him be true? How could there be –

"A second Wall?"

The adrenaline (what was left of it) sped through his veins like gasoline through a siphon, and as the siphon constricted, he could feel the Sickness stronger than ever; it was potent. "Nowhere else to go..." he had to remind himself, as he grew closer and closer to the sight before him: a large Wall that jutted out from the side of a bulky canyon-like entity, and as he continued his expedited pace, closer and closer, it soon became clearer that this was not the Wall he had once been imprisoned unto.

Though it was no different.

He reached the edge. Removing his shirt, he placed the tattered remains upon the cuffs of his tiresome wrists, and he climbed the rock, until he could feel the Wall with his tender fingertips. It was no hallucination, but it was certainly a bad dream. There are moments in life where something seems too real to be true, too clear to be a figment. On occasion, that moment will turn into dust, and it will disappear as fast as the wind is blowing. But this...this was far from a dusty fabrication.

*   *   *

Jameson arrived via chopper. The TRITE officers that were with him remained calm and quiet, hoping to mask the many, many questions they had, knowing they were not going to be answered without a bullet through the temple of clarity.

Jameson's very demeanor reeked of the Sick: his skin was cut and bloodied; sweat masked his eyes, to the point where every five seconds he found himself rubbing them with grazed fingertips; he was a mess, and he was not afraid to show it.

*   *   *

The chopper landed, as Cindy watched from her window. No older than Daniel, she was poorly positioned in a residence with her two older brothers, who were both loyal supporters of the TRITE movement. She had listened her entire life, hearing satiated phrases like: "The Sickness is within all of us", "The Sick are among the Damned and shall burn in Hell", always alleviated with a solemn, God-bearing "Amen!"...but she never took the words too seriously.

Much like Daniel, she had wondered what was outside of that Wall, and though she did not know it, her curiosity had been roused by the boy himself. In school, they were never allowed exchange of names, so the pieces never formulated a solid conclusion, but she did know she had heard many voices as a child. Only one of many made sense.

"What's outside of that Wall?" a boy had once asked his teacher, only to be slapped by a ruler upon his right hand.

"The outside is a mocking revelry of disease and death!" the teacher cited, but this boy – of whom had graduated with her, yet she never once asked his name (under allegiance, she would be killed for such a simple act) – never let up; his voice resonated within every classroom, and his question – as precise and as simple as it was – was never answered, only denied.

As Cindy watched the chopper land, she heard her brothers downstairs, as they realized there was no body with Jameson, as he had promised not even one day prior...

*   *   *

"I want everyone to remember these words: those who escape the Wall come back without their own consent. TRITE was established by the Great Admiral Sathers in an effort to maintain a balance – a balance the people of this tiresome city will never understand – and Runners are not tolerated."

*   *   *

"If Runners are not tolerated, then where's the fucking Runner now?" Cindy could hear her brother inquire downstairs. It was in this instance that two of the most loyal supporters of the TRITE Foundation that were not actual members of the movement, began to doubt, but what is "doubt" by definition?

A moment – it can be singular or plural, but it is always just one moment – where even loyalty to a system one is birthed to, trained to listen to, and willing to die for, suddenly loses its omnipotence. And Cindy could not help but think that she was not the only one watching from a window somewhere as Jameson stepped off of that chopper, noticing the body he promised to return was somehow still out there, and perhaps, he was alive.

*   *   *

"What the hell happened here?" Daniel could only wonder, as he stepped into a sea of scorched cars, all seemingly pursuing the same escape route: a single bridge that led through the Wall – an appendage Daniel had not seen at his former residence, where the Wall bared no "way out", yet it did not seem to matter, as the people of these vehicular devices did not seem to get far. The nearest to salvation: a scorched, battered red sedan, must have known what was coming.

The corpse was ducked down, skeletal arms clutching onto another body in the passenger's seat: a child, or what once was. What the blast did not kill, the radiation must have taken, as not every dead body was picked so clean of flesh; some were in the road bearing no vehicle, their skin still intact but their eyes seemed to have burned clean from their skulls, melted into veracious clumps upon the concrete, soldering like eggs on a hot plate.

Stumbling through the wreckage, suddenly the heat Daniel had felt not minutes prior had concretely dissipated, replaced by a dense fog that was cold to the touch. Though the sun had begun to rise, this town was to see no sunlight for its remainder; the gas had risen to atmospheric heights.

Suddenly he began to feel an uncomfortable shrill in

the back of his throat; he began to cough. Locating his shirt, still situated firmly upon his now-clenched fists (why they were clenched, he did not know why), he placed it over his face, feeling minor relief. Delirium, however, had already begun to settle itself within the cerebellum, and he could not help but laugh. Coughing and cackling like a witch of olden times, he made his way forward into the only building left standing (perhaps the only one that was meant to remain untouched)...

The door was already opened, and suddenly the faint sound of music began to resonate as he crept through the TRITE Headquarters of a former civilization much like his own...

CHAPTER FIFTEEN

"Sir, people are questioning as to the whereabouts of the boy..." spoke the surly officer, restraint and caution present as he dealt with precision among a well-armed Jameson, who did not respond. Staring out his window, he glanced upon a street now waking up from its nightly slumber.

"Everyone keeps calling him: 'That boy'," inquired the simply insane Admiral Jameson. "Now, why is that?"

The officer could only respond with honesty: "Well, he's just a kid, sir. He's male; he's young...so, he's a boy-"

Jameson placed a palm upon the windowsill. Rain was most surely coming; lightning struck a distant canyon, far past the Wall's restraint, but far enough for him to see – from his high-top position in the only building high enough to see over the Wall itself – as the storm moved in toward where he had just come from, not hours prior.

"...Sir?"

Jameson turned and began to pace the room.

The officer soon realized he was no longer dealing

with Jameson – the esteemed and newly-appointed Admiral – but rather, a mad man.

"I don't know where 'the boy' is, but I do know one thing: he's going to be the fall of an entire empire. He's a catalyst; a paradigm for change – change this city is not ready for..."

"But sir, you said it yourself: 'Runners will not be tolerated'. You're not even going to look for him?"

And with that, a gun was pulled from Jameson's harness. He aimed it toward the officer. "What did you learn when you were in training, officer? What did they teach you about survival?"

The officer tried his best to hide his excitement. Jameson knew what he was doing; the officer did not. "They taught us about how instinct prevails but only when not supervised. I remember they showed a video once. They showed riots in the streets, men in uniform up against a violent city...people with guns, burning their buildings, looting their stores...they showed –"

"What did that video teach you?"

Jameson cocked the weapon.

"It-it taught m-me that...that..."

"SAY IT!"

"When people are shoved too hard by the opposition, it doesn't matter what uniform you wear. You're all-for-one and one-for-all, and that guns are no use against such violence!" The officer screamed, and then he waited for the gun to shoot.

Jameson returned the pistol to his belt. "No. Bullets are no use against such violence. It is the pull of the gun, not the bullet that causes the adrenal gland to blind the weary mind." He made his way closer to the officer.

"So, we do what, exactly?"

Jameson reached for the soldier's M-16. "You better get a hell of a lot more ammunition, soldier. We start at six..."

*   *   *

As the toxins in the air began to seep through

Daniel's bloodstream, corroding his thought processes, poisoning him, dismembering the frontal lobe from the cerebellum, he wandered around the TRITE Headquarters for what seemed like hours, though it was mere minutes before he grew closer to the sound that drew him forth: a guitar, obviously set in radio format, and singing...

"I see a window and I want it painted black..."

"Hello?" Daniel murmured. His voice echoed. He followed down a narrow hallway, the walls crumbling with every step. It was clear to him that though the attack must have been meant for everything except this particular location, it did not lessen the effect of time itself; this location was very, very old.

"Hello to you, good sir!" a voice resonated over the music. Daniel jumped, hitting the wall with great impact. To his right, concealed in shadow, was a translucent figure. What appeared to be a paint roller made a sachet across a window, concealing it in a thick, black paint. The light from without was now obsolete, leaving Daniel and the stranger in darkness.

"So you're this 'Runner' everyone's been speaking of, huh? I thought you'd be taller," the man stepped into a sliver of light, revealing a can of paint in one hand, and in the other, he held the end of a paint roller, which he then dropped. He reached for a small radio to his side, which played the ominous music, the words all about painting things black. The man's silhouette stopped only close enough for Daniel to see the mechanism; he remained in darkness - it felt as if he had a purpose. Daniel tried to step closer, but the man outstretched his free hand.

"That's close enough, Mister Sathers. I would have thought a son of the great Admiral who once ran this place would be taller, bulkier...when I heard on the HAM radio's one and only living channel that, yet another member of that wretched family had escaped his cage like a parakeet in flight, I figured he'd be coming here, of all places..."

He gestured his free hand toward the fresh paint scattered all across the walls, windows, doorways...it seemed the entire building was coated in black paint. "So I decided I'd do some painting..."

Daniel was now scared and confused. "Who are you?"

The man laughed at such a sad question.

"My boy, I'm you!"

"So, you're a time traveler?" Daniel stated satirically. The man laughed once more, cackling.

"No, you fucking idiot! You Sathers' are all the fucking same: you have such a solid grasp on the idea of control that you forget to think before you speak," and so he returned to painting, the radio resetting as the song ended, and then began to play it again. It was on a loop.

"You know why they banned this music, kid? It made people think," he said as he rolled paint across another window, slowly formulating a cloud of darkness within the room; the sun crept through the small cracks he had missed, but it seemed this vagabond had all the time in the world to check his work.

He turned to face Daniel. "It's hard to train a herd of sheep when they know how to think. To maintain control, you must have the control to maintain and to keep such a livid entity as the human being trained like sheep, you must keep it numb, stupefied..."

He rolled another layer of paint, humming to the song...

This man knew something. So many questions rolled before Daniel's eyes: who was this man? Why was he alive? Was he a member of TRITE? And if not, what was he doing here?

"I know you have questions, and they'll be answered soon enough. But for now..." the man tossed a brush in Daniel's direction. "Care to help me out here? The sun's rising rather fast this feeble dawn, and the radiation is stronger when hit by direct sunlight..."

CHAPTER SIXTEEN

"This won't do," Cindy talked erratically to herself as she prepared for her day at work. Waiting tables was no dream job. Her dream had been to grow up to become a great TRITE leader, but it soon became clear through years of mind-numbing memorization of TRITE's "25 Points of Ethical Conduct" that women were not allowed to become so much as a member of the organization, let alone a leader among a throng of wolves. Her place was in modern-day society, if this was what "modern-day" was to be defined as.

She threw on a red shirt, black jeans, and headed out of the door, noticing a clock above the doorway that it was 8:59am. She had exactly one minute to get from her house to the diner downtown, and as women were not allowed to drive, it would be on-foot. It would be her third strike, and she was facing a harsh firing.

But her predisposed notion of the phrase: "firing" was nothing in comparison to what she was about to witness. As she reached for the doorknob, an uneasy feeling crept into her stomach. Something was not right...where were her brothers? And that was when the door blew open, and smoke enveloped the kitchen as she was thrust to the ground by a squadron of TRITE officers. Guns were swift in their drawing, and she cringed as cold metal pressed upon her cheek...

*   *   *

It was hours before Daniel and the man in shadow so much as spoke a word to one another. But with nowhere else to go, and no refuge except a binding trust in a man he had just met, he kept painting, moving from window to window, until all sunlight was gone. Then, the room was suddenly lit as the man began to spark candles (the smoke reacted with the radiation, causing a neon-green glow that shrouded the room).

The song reset for a fortieth time.

Finally, the man pulled up a chair, and he sat. He gestured for Daniel to do the same. And so there they were – Daniel, now a fugitive in the name of TRITE, and a man who, for all he knew, was an operative waiting for Jameson to arrive. Then again, the eccentricity of this man was nothing close to what would be expected from TRITE. They were clean-cut, well-shaven, and most importantly, they never smiled.

On the flip side, the man before him was shoddy, his hair long and scraggly, his eyes reddened, and no TRITE insignia was branded on his forearm...and a timid smile never left his face, bearing yellowed teeth. He was no

TRITE operative, but that only brought up the question at hand: how did he know who Daniel was?

As he lit a cigarette, the man in shadow gave his name. "You can call me Paul...or Randal, or John, or Smith. It doesn't matter. I've been here so fucking long that I can't even remember the letter it started with, let alone the full connotation."

"My name's Daniel, though I assume you must already know that. Mind you, I must ask: how do you know who I am, Mister...Smith?"

The man flicked the match – still lit – against a wall to the side, where the flame met with the drying paint and the two coalesced, almost igniting before it burned into ash. "I was like you once. I was a Runner," he inhaled on the cigarette, holding the smoke in his lungs, intoxicating his throat, before releasing a wave of smoke.

"I don't know the entire story, Daniel. I don't know why you ran, or what caused you to run, but I do know this: you had every God-given right to run, and it is our purpose – as human beings – to run when we smell danger..."

"It wasn't my intention to run –"

Smith cut him off. "Oh, I know damned well. No 'Runner' is ever destined to run, but that is the beauty of it: they call us 'Runners' because we escaped, not because we ran. If that were the case, they'd be shooting every citizen of your former New Manhattan that peddled a bicycle faster than ten miles-per-hour. We aren't 'Runners'; we are escapers, and that is why we hide."

Daniel glanced around, reminding himself of where he was: the ruins of a town surrounded by a great wall. He also reminded himself that everything except for the building he was now entombed in was blasted into smithereens. "What happened here?"

Smith finished the cigarette, tossing it to the ground and snuffing it with his foot (noted: he had no shoes). "War happened. You can just go ahead and assume, for now, that you were not the only one who had once seen too much."

Bizarre as it was, Daniel felt a strong connection to this man, almost as if they were family. Somewhere deep inside of his gut, he could feel that they shared blood, or at the least, they had both shed blood in the name of instinct, but why was that?

"Were you the one who 'saw too much'?" Daniel

inquired, and Smith laughed; he seemed to always laugh.

"I'll put it this way..." he leaned in, his wrists meeting with his lap. "I may have run; I may have survived the very Holocaust that took place here some odd years ago...but I never escaped. These walls speak to me every goddamned day, Daniel. They scream: 'Murderer'...other times, they scream: 'Saint'. All I know is, at least one voice may be correct..."

The barometric pressure in the room seemed to drop, as an icy wind blew through the halls like a ghost. Smith stood up. "That wind...it always reminds me of why I'm here..."

*   *   *

"Do you know why you are here, Cindy?" asked a voice to her right. She could not see through the black tarnish that was now over her head; she could barely breathe through its confinement, let alone answer the question. A firm wallop to the back of her dome with the butt of an M-16 threw her from the chair, and she was thrust to the ground, but as her arms and legs were tied, she could not rise; she could not stand.

"Please...just let me go!" she pleaded, but her time here was to be decided only by an answer she could not provide.

"We have detailed records that you were once a student at Denison Middle School, correct?" the voice to her right inquired. She tried to stand, but she was knocked back down by yet another blow to the temporal lobe. She found the strength to speak:

"I was there." She coughed up blood, but it did not spill onto the floor; it remained within the black bag, only enhancing due diligence to vomit.

"So you were in a classroom, multiple times, with Subject 'Daniel A. Sathers', correct?"

"I don't know! We aren't allowed to know!"

"The fear is alive in you," a voice to the left sauntered.

"Just kill her. She's of no use," another voice.

"No! We need this one. She knows where he is!"

Cindy entreated once more: "Please, let me go!"

It was then that she was grabbed by the shoulder, repositioned upon the chair, and the black bag was removed. Looking around, she was in what appeared to be something similar to an old-fashioned interrogation room, like the ones she had only seen on television screens: a one-way mirror, a single table centered, and several armed guards at her sides.

"Why am I here?" she asked, the blood clotting from her now-missing front tooth.

"Again, I'll ask you: do you know the whereabouts of Daniel A. Sathers? We know that you were involved in multiple classroom activities with the boy. He's now a Federal Threat, Level Six. Do you know what that means, Cindy?"

She decided it was best to not speak, as the Sickness was growing livid within her veins. The silence seemed to only piss off Jameson more. He grabbed for one of the soldier's M-16s and pointed the muzzle square against her forehead.

"You're dead one way or another, Cindy. Just answer the fucking question!" He bent down to meet her eye-to-eye. "I know you're afraid; I know the Sickness is rising in you, and I would have shot you on-sight if I didn't suspect you know something. Your very testament will set you free. Now –"

The gun cocked. "Tell the fucking truth!"

*   *   *

Daniel listened for what seemed like hours, as Smith elaborated on the situation. Nuclear war was all he gathered. The conversation ended when the sound of a helicopter high above caused an odd sentiment in Smith. "They're still looking for me. They'll never find me...but they'll just keep on fucking looking. Do you know what it's like to live your life in a constant state of paranoia?"

Daniel could only chuckle. "I thought you said you knew who I was. What kind of stupid question is that?!"

Smith did not laugh; he did not respond. His eyes had risen, peering through a window he had painted in black paint hours prior. He obviously could not see through it, but in his mind, perhaps, he thought he could.

"Did you ever read past Page 217, Daniel?"

A nerve was struck. How did he know?

"Page 218 is where the magic lies," spoke Smith, as he removed from his side the same book Daniel was carrying with him in a single knapsack he brought with him. He checked it, realizing he was low on water. If this man had managed to survive nuclear Holocaust, perhaps he had provisions.

"Do you have any water?" Daniel inquired.

Smith rose. "Don't follow me," he said as he exited the room. The wind blew ice through the room once more, and Daniel shivered; the hair on the back of his neck rose, as suddenly he could hear the voices:

"Murderer...Saint...Murderer...Saint..."

It was interrupted by Smith, tossing a six-pack of bottled water toward Daniel. "Go nuts," he said, as he returned to his seat. "TRITE made sure to protect this particular establishment when they sautéed the rest of the city with gas and bombs. I never knew why, until I found what they were keeping in here.

It's much more than bottled water. Everything you need to know about TRITE, your father's poignant massacres on multiple cities, and the very reason TRITE was formed, is all on record, and if it had any merit I'd show you but all you truly need to know is this..."

Smith opened to Page 218. "Read!"

CHAPTER SEVENTEEN

Days passed, yet Cindy did not budge. Water boarded, electrocuted, and beaten, she had decided somewhere around the second day of her confinement that this was it: her death was to lie at the end of a loaded gun, simply for not being able to answer a question she did not understand. Why did they assume she knew this Runner, and was she the only one sitting in this desolate prison, facing interrogation for something she knew nothing about?

It occurred to her that her brothers must have noticed by now that she was missing. What would they do? What would the people do if she was somehow released back into society? Above all else, why did they choose her? Then it hit her – not the butt of a gun, but the realization that perhaps she did know this boy.

"Are you ready to answer, Cindy?" Jameson said as she was dragged by her wrists into the interrogation room, the floor being hosed down of old blood she had shed in the name of terror. And then Jameson heard an answer he was not prepared for.

"I don't know him, but I met him. I can't be sure, but it has to be him. It has to be!"

Jameson was in shock. This was not what he was expecting. He was expecting for this girl to die, so he could drag her through the streets, dead and bloodied, as a warning to the residents of New Manhattan that if anybody had any information as to the whereabouts of Daniel, they would be killed.

The last thing he expected was to actually locate someone – Cindy: one of fifty others currently being interrogated – who had any idea who this boy was. It took a few moments to respond... "What was he like, Cindy? Any information you provide will allow us to set you free. Just tell us: what do you feel kept him up at night?"

Cindy's next words were chilling, even to a man who had no pulse, no heart, and above all else: no emotion. "He was curious. He always asked about the outside world..."

Jameson nodded to one of the TRITE officers to his side, and Cindy's ropes were cut. "You're coming with us, Cindy..."

*   *   *

Daniel read page 218 – an unsettling, tiresome read. "This can't be true..."

Smith rose, peering once more through a window he could not see through. His voice was solemn. "Yes, it's quite true."

Daniel rose, too, rising behind Smith, standing before a man who perhaps was once in a situation much like his own; quite a paradox, or was it a paradigm? "Tell me...did you suffer the same atrocities I suffered?"

Smith did not turn. "Years ago, before they shredded this town of life, I witnessed a young boy minding his own business, kicking rocks in the street, when suddenly one of those rocks accidentally butted against a rogue TRITE officer. The poignant bastard took it personal. The boy was so young, Daniel, that he did not know of his crime; he had no idea what was coming..."

Smith reflected...

"The officer was under command of a man you once knew as your father. Last I heard that son-of-a-bitch was murdered in cold blood, and I hate to say this to his own blood, but he got what he deserved. Karma, Daniel, is an essence of life. It exists. But it wasn't the fact that the officer shot that poor child that caused what was to come..."

Daniel could feel the ice rise within the room. Shivering, he noticed Smith was still; he was either so used to this swing in temperature, or perhaps Daniel was the only one feeling it. Smith continued.

"Next thing I knew, I was standing over the body of a dead TRITE officer. I never even caught his name. All I remember is a hammer stained in blood, and a dead man. But what truly caused the events that came, was not my actions. It was when your father tried to cover the act as malicious intent," Smith turned to face Daniel. "You, too, have seen the tepid hands of murder. You, too, know how good it feels to let instinct prevail when necessary. That was what caused it..."

Images flashed before Smith's eyes, as suddenly the black paint formed pictorials of a time not long ago, as he was hunted through the Forbidden Lands like a deer straying from a herd. He watched in third person as he was beaten, then dragged through the streets in an almost sacrificial manner. "You see, Daniel, the human being – deep down inside – wants to see blood. Why do you think they spend so much fucking time 'controlling' the masses of your town...and once my town, with vagabond lies about this 'Sickness'? Why do you think they require such control? And once more –"

The song reset for a fiftieth time. "I see a window and I want it painted black..." Smith turned and kicked the side of the radio, until the tape scrambled. He opened the cassette player and handed the cassette to Daniel. "Why on God's once-green earth would they ban this song? Because thoughts in a place like this are forbidden. You are alone. You are me!"

*   *   *

Cindy's brothers were perhaps the first to exit their homes as New Manhattan's automated speaker system called for: "All eyes and ears" to exit from their daily activities, and peer upon a desolate street. It was there that TRITE had gathered, in almost a ceremonial fashion, marching forward with M-16s in hand, and behind them was a large hammer of a vehicle. Ropes were attached at the back end, with fifteen dead bodies dragging behind it. Their blood smeared the concrete as the bullet wounds in their heads perforated fresh crimson. Jameson stood at the top of the vehicle with a loud horn in hand.

"The Sickness will not be tolerated! Do you see what your city has become? Do you see what happens when you protect an escaped convict?!" he screamed, his madness now quite lucid.

Then Cindy's brothers saw it: Cindy's corpse, among the fifteen, was brutally beaten, her arms and legs twisting as they frayed against the dark pavement.

"CINDY!" one screamed, but with the crowd that had gathered, his voice was drowned out. And perhaps that was the moment when a city built upon a foundation of lies, deceit, and above all else: the shedding of innocent blood, was no longer within the tolerance of the two most loyal supporters of the supposed TRITE Foundation.

*   *   *

"Lies will not be tolerated! The SICKNESS will not be –" but Jameson was unable to finish his sentence that cold morning, as something began to occur at the front of his escapade. His only thought – the last thought he would ever think – was so simple in nature yet so equally complex: "Why are they shooting?"

Cindy's eldest brother was shot through the arm, though it was unnoticed by Jameson. It really did not matter, as even without a working arm, perhaps the human is blessed with two arms for such a purpose as the raising of a disarmed officer's own rifle, and the proper aligning of a single bullet, as it grazed through Jameson's right temple, and blood emptied through the loud horn as he fell backward, landing next to Cindy's body.

CHAPTER EIGHTEEN

"You better use my car, Daniel. It's stuck in gridlock, but it's a red Corolla, much like the one used to kill your father. You can't miss it; it's the only one with inflated tires."

Daniel was caught off-guard by Smith's words, as the man tossed him a set of car keys. "Drive home, Daniel. You don't want to miss the fireworks..."

*   *   *

And so Daniel sped back, passing Mile 106 with a steadfast pace. He could hear the voices once more: "Murderer...Saint..." He shook his head. As he raced back toward home, he realized that perhaps this seemingly self-centered time warp he was in was merely a repeating entity. And so he reached back, feeling around the back seat. And there it was: an M-16, just like in Donnie's truck. He put it upon his lap; he knew it would have purpose, and just like Donnie's, he knew this one was loaded.

*   *   *

Cindy's brother approached one of the officers, as the townspeople – suddenly staring down dozens of armed and loaded rifles – rushed the danger in a silhouette. For once, they did run, and it was not in the other direction; with hands like snakes, they stripped TRITE of their weapons, and one-by-one, inch-by-inch, order fell upon opposing shoulders.

Cindy's brother stared into the eyes of the officer before him. Dilated pupils, sweat upon his brow, and fear coursing through his veins and into his heart, Cindy's brother could only laugh, realizing that the paradigm shift was now broken; the people were holding the guns, and the officers were Sick...

He jumped to the top of the vehicle, as others untied the ropes that strung the corpses, and Cindy's body was taken into the arms of her other brother, who cried, tears meshing with the blood. And that was it. The eldest – the one atop the vehicle – picked up the loud horn (blood emptying from its nozzle) and spoke into its crimson-stained end. The loud horn beckoned: "These TRITE officers are now under arrest under sanctity of their sacred Plaguta Armada. Kill them for their sins."

And so the town did as asked by their new leader, shooting down a good one-hundred TRITE officers in the name of "being Sick". And then suddenly all fell still, among a sea of corpses, all slain under the very disease they were trained to protect.

*   *   *

There was one survivor, much like in the case of the Main Street Massacre (upon which Sathers' body now lay in ashes), only this time, it was a TRITE official named James. Having dodged his way out of the cesspool of carnage that was taking place all around him – rioters, bricks and mortars tossed and sullying the street with fresh blood, and guns – he stripped of his uniform and made his way as a casual civilian into Jameson's office.

He scurried around the desk, looking for a crucial something Jameson had entrusted upon him if he were ever to be decimated (in this case: shot through the head).

"Damnit, where is it?!" he screamed in frenzy, as the

sound of rioters growing closer came into earshot. He looked out the window, and he could see them now: the people of the town he was trained to protect for so long, now in upheaval. They were making their way forward, toward the TRITE Foundation headquarters, in an almost surrealistic fashion (the only things missing at this point were torches and pitchforks).

Finally, he located the codes in one of the lower drawers in Jameson's desk. He made his way to the telephone, and he dialed a number.

"This is Lieutenant Peterson, representing Admiral Clause Sathers...yes? Correct, he is no longer with us. The city is in crisis; the Sick are everywhere! We need a full cleanse...huh? Of course I have the launch codes. Tell me when ready..."

*   *   *

Smith's car had broken down some odd hours ago, so Daniel simply abandoned everything except for the book, and the gun, and began walking. Too tired to care, he passed Mile 9. He could see the corn maize he had crawled through; he could see bullet shells every which-way; he could see the Wall, proud and valiant...but something wasn't right...

Two cars sped past him, pushing 90 miles per hour. Then, two more. They were rushing from the city, and not the other way around, which was quite bizarre, taking into consideration that there is no way outside of the Wall without doing as Daniel had done: climbing over the very entity itself. How on God's torn earth could vehicles have made it out with no exit big enough to leave?

It was then that Daniel remembered Page 218...

"Oh, no..." And that was it.

His second (no, third) wind took hold; he grew figurative wings, and he soared closer to his former home, and the closer he got, the worse things sounded, the worse things smelled. He could see the smoke billowing from beyond the encompassment of the Wall. Then he saw them: large, domineering jets, swooping toward the city in a torrent of flight. He knew what was about to happen; he had read about Hiroshima. Maybe one day, people would read about New Manhattan, too.

CHAPTER NINETEEN

Three years later…

Sidney could not believe what he was seeing. The same Wall as his own town, only it was decimated at the base. He entered the abandoned city with caution. Making his way past abandoned cars and a street lined with corpses, he heard an odd tune.

He made his way closer and closer, until he found himself staring upward at the ever-so-mighty TRITE Headquarters: the only building untouched by what appeared to have been a nuclear fallout. He entered, and suddenly he could hear humming.

"I see a window and I want it painted black..."

Sidney turned a corner, and an odd figure stood among the darkness, with a paint roller in one hand, smearing black paint across one of the windows of a dust-ridden room. The man, quiet in his actions, turned.

And it was then that Daniel stepped out from within the shadows, and greeted his new protégé...

"You know why they banned this song, kid? Because it made people think. A herd of sheep is harder to train..."

THROUGH JADED EYES
RYAN W. McCLELLAN

VISIT ME ONLINE

The QR code below can be scanned with your iPhone's camera. It will take you to my official website, and I would appreciate it if you took the time to check out my other books. A new novel will be released every 3 months, and I would love it if you signed up for my email mailing list.

ABOUT THE AUTHOR

Ryan W. McClellan, MS, was born in vibrant Miami, Florida. He has been weaving stories for as long as he can remember. He has six captivating books gracing store shelves and a collection of free eBooks available to readers worldwide. McClellan has established himself as a versatile and passionate storyteller. His journey as an author began at just seventeen, when he penned his first novel. It was a milestone that cemented his lifelong love for writing. Over the years, his dedication to the craft has earned him recognition, including awards for his compelling stories.

www.Rwmcc.com
www.Facebok.com/Rwmcc

INTERESTED YET?

If you liked this book, check out my others! They can be found using the same QR code as before, but I figured I'd include these regardless. These are my older books but be prepared for new novels over my lifetime.

Purchase on Amazon.com!

PLEASE LEAVE A REVIEW!

Being an author is tough. It would mean the world to me if you took the time to leave a positive review. I am not allowed to link anything directly to Amazon, but I would appreciate an honest review if you enjoyed this book. Scan this QR code with your iPhone to leave a review! Whether good or bad, I want to hear your input. It is feedback, and it helps a starving author!

WANT TO PREORDER?

If you are interested in preordering, scan the QR code below to visit my dedicated page to future releases, fill out the form, and I will add you to my mailing list and keep you updated! Those marked with "Preorder Status" get a free copy before release, and act as beta readers, i.e. you get to review me!

www.ingramcontent.com/pod-product-compliance
Lightning Source LLC
Chambersburg PA
CBHW050512160726
48003CB00001B/267